Samuel French Acting Edition

M000039877

Sorry!
Wrong Chimney!

by Jack Sharkey
and Leo W. Sears

‖ SAMUEL FRENCH ‖

SAMUELFRENCH.COM   SAMUELFRENCH.CO.UK

FOR PRODUCTION ENQUIRIES

UNITED STATES AND CANADA
Info@SamuelFrench.com
1-866-598-8449

UNITED KINGDOM AND EUROPE
Plays@SamuelFrench.co.uk
020-7255-4302

Each title is subject to availability from Samuel French, depending
upon country of performance. Please be aware that *SORRY! WRONG
CHIMNEY!* may not be licensed by Samuel French in your territory.
Professional and amateur producers should contact the nearest Samuel
French office or licensing partner to verify availability.

MUSIC USE NOTE

Licensees are solely responsible for obtaining formal written permission from copyright owners to use copyrighted music in the performance of this play and are strongly cautioned to do so. If no such permission is obtained by the licensee, then the licensee must use only original music that the licensee owns and controls. Licensees are solely responsible and liable for all music clearances and shall indemnify the copyright owners of the play(s) and their licensing agent, Samuel French, against any costs, expenses, losses and liabilities arising from the use of music by licensees. Please contact the appropriate music licensing authority in your territory for the rights to any incidental music.

IMPORTANT BILLING AND CREDIT REQUIREMENTS

If you have obtained performance rights to this title, please refer to your licensing agreement for important billing and credit requirements.

SORRY! WRONG CHIMNEY! had its World Premiere at the Metro Playhouse Dinner Theatre in Phoenix, Arizona, on November 1st, 1989, with the following players and personnel:

DAVID..........................Thomas M. Dvorak
SAMANTHA ....Rachel Underwood
NATALIE............................ Karen Lugosi
WILLIAM...................... Gary W. Charlson
KRIS ....Ed Cole
SHEILA.................................Robyn Allen
POLICEMAN .... Brad Garday

Director/Producer	Leo W. Sears
Ass't. Director/Lights/Sound	Larry Swanson
Business Manager	Jan Sears
Group Sales	Wes Norton

CHARACTERS

DAVID TUTTLE, a struggling young executive
SAMANTHA TUTTLE, his bride of 6 months
NATALIE WELDON, their neighbor across the
   hall
WILLIAM WELDON, Natalie's psychiatrist
   husband
KRIS KREIGLE, a man with a Holiday delusion
SHEILA, Kris's doggedly devoted fiancee
POLICEMAN, a determined disciple of Law and
   Order

The entire action of the play takes place in the
   Tuttles' metropolitan apartment

ACT I
Early evening, ten days before Christmas

ACT II
About 2 1/2 seconds later

ACT III
One hour later

ACT I

SCENE: The apartment of DAVID and SAMANTHA
  TUTTLE. It is modern, sparsely decorated, but
  comfortable. Stage Right has upstage exit to kitchen;
  Stage Left has door to apartment hallway upstage, door
  to bedroom downstage; against right wall below the
  doorway is a small table holding telephone and stereo;
  upstage wall has fireplace and small, partly decorated,
  Christmas tree. A sofa center stage has a long-and-
  narrow coffee table before it.

[NOTE: The foregoing is the ideal set, to be augmented
  with pictures on walls, perhaps a window in the upstage
  wall with snow packed against its lower corners,
  additional chairs as desired. However: The Metro
  Playhouse stage dimensions at the Phoenix premiere
  were such that a modified version of the setting was
  used (see Set Design) and it functioned admirably well;
  the Christmas tree, on this smaller stage, was a
  miniature one upon the desk downstage right, which
  also held the stereo. The downstage-facing fireplace was
  just big enough for KRIS to almost fit into during his
  vain escape try; the relative positions of the bedroom
  and hall doors in this smaller set made KRIS's final exit
  somewhat extended—but it also extended the hilarity of
  the moment.]

AT RISE: SAMANTHA, an attractive woman in her early
  20s, wearing red pajamas and a Santa hat, brings several
  boxes out of the bedroom and places them on sofa, then
  exits to kitchen and returns with a pair of wine glasses

7

which she places on coffee table; she then goes to light
switch near hall door and DIMS ROOM LIGHTS, then
turns on some Christmas MUSIC on stereo.
DOORBELL RINGS. She goes to door, striking
romantic pose as she flings it open on:

SAMANTHA. Ho-ho-ho, baby! (*NATALIE, a well-*
endowed woman in her 30s, enters in flamboyant dress)

NATALIE. Ho-ho-ho, yourself, Sam! You been hitting
the eggnog early?

SAMANTHA. (*rueful laugh*) Sorry, Natalie, I thought
you were David. Come in, come in! (*will un-dim switch*
and LIGHTS COME UP FULL as she closes door)

NATALIE. Maybe I shouldn't. I mean, if you're about
to pounce on David in your pajamas—?

SAMANTHA. Believe me, anything that happened
would still get a G-rating! (*waves her downstage a bit*)

NATALIE. (*moving down to sofa area.*) A G-rating,
with the two of you practically still on your honeymoon?

SAMANTHA. (*turns music off*) Not practically.
Theoretically.

NATALIE. So what's this pajama bit?

SAMANTHA. (*crosses to sofa, sits*) The honeymoon's
kind of—worn off. David's been working nights *and*
weekends, lately. A lot. He *does* come home for dinner, but
then he pops right out again.

NATALIE. You think red pajamas might put a little
glue under his shoes?

SAMANTHA. Well, that and—maybe—decorating the
tree tonight—listening to Christmas carols while we
worked—and doubling the rum in the eggnog!

NATALIE. (*sits beside her on sofa, on:*) Well, if
nothing else, you'd send him back to work *jolly!*

SAMANTHA. What *happens* to men after you marry
them?!

NATALIE. I'm not sure. If you ever find out, let *me* know, and I'll figure out what's wrong with me and Bill! How long *have* you been married, now—five months?

SAMANTHA. Six. And already he'd rather be at the office than here with me.

NATALIE. He's got to come home to bed sometime!

SAMANTHA. Yeah. To sleep!

NATALIE. Sam, honey, you're taking this too hard. Men are ambitious. In a big company like David's, putting in extra hours is the way to *advance* up the ranks. Once he's a top executive, he can let somebody *else* put in the overtime.

SAMANTHA. But can I *wait* that long?

NATALIE. (*shrugs*) What *else* have you got to do? Say, by the way—do you *have* any of that double-rum eggnog handy?

SAMANTHA. (*starts to get up*) I have all the *ingredients* ready—only take a minute to whip it up ...

NATALIE. (*stops her*) Ah, don't bother. Why should *I* get jolly when Bill is across the hall sound *asleep!*

SAMANTHA. Isn't it a little *early* for bedtime?

NATALIE. Oh, it's just a nap after work. He says listening to his patients drone on and on all day *almost* puts him to sleep, but he hangs on till he gets home. I'll wake him up for dinner.

SAMANTHA. And then, I'll bet, you get terribly romantic, don't you!

NATALIE. Well—*I* do, for all the good it does me.

SAMANTHA. Bill's not in the mood, either? Just like David?

NATALIE. Not while there's anything running in prime time. Oh, he *cuddles* nicely on the sofa, but I can't get it to go much farther than that—nothing that involves his taking his eyes off the TV screen, anyhow.

SAMANTHA. I'm *so* glad!

NATALIE. You're *what?*

SAMANTHA. Oh, I mean, so glad that David's not the *only* unromantic husband in the building. At least your Bill is *home* with you nights, and not out with—I mean—not *out* ...

NATALIE. Say, you *do* have a problem! You're not being silly enough to imagine David has—how can I put it?—something "on the side?"

SAMANTHA. Oh, if only I were sure I *was* imagining!

NATALIE. But honey—David is *bananas* about you! You're all he thinks about, all he talks about!

SAMANTHA. (*a little frown*) How do *you* know so much about what David thinks and talks about?

NATALIE. Sam, I meet your husband almost every day!

SAMANTHA. Natalie, what are you saying?!

NATALIE. Relax, Samantha, relax! I don't mean I *meet* David daily—I mean, almost every day, I meet *David.* There's a difference.

SAMANTHA. It—it does sound better with the different stress ...

NATALIE. Look, honey, this apartment building has hallways, and mailboxes in the lobby, and a pool and Jacuzzi out back, and a newsstand on the corner, and—it's not too unlikely for me and David to run into one another now and again, is it?

SAMANTHA. I—I guess not.

NATALIE. Good. And when we meet, as friendly neighbors, we talk. And when David talks, he talks about *you!* Oh, *I* talk, too, mostly about Bill—but all *m y* comments are complaints. David's are nothing but compliments.

SAMANTHA. You're just saying that to make me feel better.

NATALIE. True. But also because it's a fact. (*stands*) There, now do you feel better?

SAMANTHA. You know—I *do*. Much better. (*stands*) Thanks, Natalie. (*starts with her, toward door*) Your visit has done me a world of good.

NATALIE. (*stops*) Oh! Silly me! I almost forgot the *reason* for the visit! The sight of you in those romantic pajamas must have startled it right out of my head.

SAMANTHA. This wasn't just a social call?

NATALIE. More a *duty* call, as friend and neighbor. Honey—now don't get upset or anything, but—have you heard about the Santa Claus burglar?

SAMANTHA. Of *course* I have. Nothing *else* in the news, lately!

NATALIE. But did you hear he's been seen not two blocks from here?

SAMANTHA. *No! That* I didn't know. Oh, dear, now I'm more worried than *ever* about David being out nights!

NATALIE. Now-now, it's perfectly safe if you keep your door locked—unless that fireplace has a *wide* chimney—?

SAMANTHA. (*looks that way*) Not—not *very* wide ... unless —just how *big* is this burglar, anyhow?

NATALIE. Hard to *tell* a guy's build in a Santa suit. Could be all fluff and padding around a body skinny as a snake. Maybe the best course is to keep a *fire* going all night long.

SAMANTHA. It's really a shame. Spoils the Christmas spirit, kind of, a guy dressed like Santa breaking into people's apartments. He must be sick.

NATALIE. I know. Just my luck, he'd pop into *our* place and my heroic Bill would lie him down and start *analyzing* him!

SAMANTHA. (*laughs*) That's what psychiatrists are for, Natalie.

NATALIE. Personally, I'd just as soon cure him of his criminal tendencies the speedier way—with a baseball bat!

SAMANTHA. Bill's way would be better—you could *charge* him for the cure!

NATALIE. Hmm, never thought of that! Well, either way, Bill and I are ready for him, and he'll get what he deserves.

SAMANTHA. What a person like that deserves is a lump of *coal* for Christmas!

NATALIE. In his stocking?

SAMANTHA. Upside of his head! (*BOTH laugh; then:*)

NATALIE. Well, honey, you just keep this door locked tight, and if you hear anything in the night when David's not here, just give a holler and I'll charge right over with that baseball bat—I can't really expect Bill to charge over toting the *couch!*

SAMANTHA. (*laughs, opening door*) Thanks, Natalie, I'll keep it in mind. And Natalie—thanks.

NATALIE. (*smiles*) What are friends for? (*exits; SAMANTHA closes door after her, SAMANTHA sits and starts going through boxes, looking at ornaments and decorations. One of the boxes she opens has Santa costume in it. She opens it just as DAVID enters. She just gets a quick glimpse of it, and its presence doesn't register. DAVID is a handsome young executive in his mid-twenties. He wears overcoat as he enters. He is wearing suit and tie under. SAMANTHA rushes to him, knocking over boxes as she does, and embraces him. In midst of embrace, DAVID spots Santa suit which was spilled with rest of decorations. He breaks free, almost knocking SAMANTHA over as he does. He rushes to Santa costume and quickly stuffs it back into box.*)

DAVID. (*almost breathless*) Well, Sam, what's going on? (*nonchalantly hiding box behind back*)

SAMANTHA. (*crossing to him*) I thought we could have a romantic evening. Just the two of us decorating the tree and the apartment.

DAVID. Oh, honey, that sounds—just wonderful! But—

SAMANTHA. David, *please* don't tell me you have to go back to the office tonight!

DAVID. Sam, if I *don't* tell you that—how *will* I explain when I go out?

SAMANTHA. Awww, David!

DAVID. (*backing toward door, box still hidden*) I know, I know, and I promise you, soon as Christmas is over, I'll be the most romantic husband in this apartment building!

SAMANTHA. From what I've heard, *that's* not saying much! (*starts to cry, rushes into bedroom, slams door*)

DAVID. (*lamely*) *Hon-ee* ...?! (*slumps*) Oh, hell. (*shakes head, swings box around to hold it in front of him, now, turns and opens front door, then steps back in panic as NATALIE steps in; he whips box behind his back from her, instantly, forces a smile, and:*) Why—Natalie! How nice!

NATALIE. If you *really* think it's nice, you should tell the sweat glands on your forehead.

DAVID. (*wipes cuff across brow*) Hot. Very hot in this apartment. Like an oven.

NATALIE. David, what are you being so *nervous* about?

DAVID. Wh—what m—makes you think I'm b—being nervous? (*croaks an unconvincing laugh*)

NATALIE. You don't *always* talk like Mel Tillis.

DAVID. Like M—m—m—m—m—m—?

NATALIE. You *said* it! Or *tried* to, anyhow.

DAVID. (*mastering himself*) Just the heat. Heat always makes me stutter.

NATALIE. You must have a hell of a time in Hawaii!
... Where the humahumanukanuka-apuahua goes
swimming by?

DAVID. L–look, was there something you wanted? I'm
in a kind of hurry ...

NATALIE. More overtime money for Christmas?

DAVID. Damn, I wish they *paid* executives overtime!
That'd simplify *everything!*

NATALIE. You mean all these late hours of yours are
for *nothing?*

DAVID. Look, only *clerical* people get overtime pay.
Executives get the same money if they work fifteen hours a
day or *none*. Sometimes I wish I *weren't* on the corporate
ladder—!

NATALIE. Then why knock yourself out this way?
You can't be an *inefficient* executive, can you?

DAVID. Of course not!

NATALIE. So how come you can't get your work done
by quitting time?

DAVID. Natalie, is there some reason you're asking so
many questions about my personal business?

NATALIE. (*looks around, sees they're alone, draws him
a bit into the room, speaks conspiratorially:*) Darn right
there is! David, as a friend, I should tell you something –
something important.

DAVID. (*at sea*) This—this isn't about my *deodorant*,
is it?

NATALIE. You smell just dandy. A little sweaty, but
dandy. No, it's about Sam.

DAVID. (*glances toward bedroom*) She's—all right,
isn't she?

NATALIE. Haven't you seen her tonight?

DAVID. Just briefly. She seemed—upset.

NATALIE. David, she *is* upset. Listen—(*lowers her
voice even more:*) I'm only telling you this because I think

the two of you are such a swell couple, and I wouldn't want anything to change that.

DAVID. Telling me *what*—? *(has unconsciously lowered his own voice to her conspiratorial level)*

NATALIE. Samantha thinks—or is on the *brink* of thinking—that there's—well—maybe another woman!

DAVID. *(normal volume:)* WHAT?!

NATALIE. Ssssh! *(pulls him farther into center of room)* Keep your voice down! It's these late night *hours* of yours, and no romance on the home front. It's a bit extreme, but I can't exactly blame her. You *are* really working nights, aren't you—?

DAVID. Scout's honor, yes! *(glances at bedroom door; then:)* Except—

NATALIE. Except what?

DAVID. *(very low-voiced:)* I'm not working at my *office!*

NATALIE. *(normal volume:)* WHAT?!

DAVID. Ssssh! *(pulls her farther into room)* Keep your voice down!

NATALIE. Sorry.

DAVID. *(extends box) This* is what I've been doing nights! At Carmichael's Department Store!

NATALIE. *(peeks into box, reacts)* You've been playing Santa?!

DAVID. I want to get Sam a present—a terrific present—her very first Christmas present from me since our wedding! And—I can't *afford* it!

NATALIE. On an *executive's* salary?

DAVID. Don't let the title fool you. I'm still on the Entry Level. I make peanuts compared to the *big* bosses. And what with gas for the car, keeping my suits cleaned and pressed, the rent on this apartment, not to mention food bills, and—

NATALIE. (*impatiently*) I *get* it, I *get* it! And I must say, I'm impressed. Working all day at the office, then working all night with tiny little screaming demons on your knee—

DAVID. (*moving doorward*) And I'll lose *that* job if I don't get *out* of here—!

NATALIE. (*moving along with him*) Sam would be so proud of you if she knew—

DAVID. (*stops*) She *mustn't* know!

NATALIE. Why not?

DAVID. Because if she found out, she'd say she'd rather have *me* at *home* nights than *any* present, and I'd have to quit! And what a dreary Christmas morning there'd be, *then*, with nothing under the tree ...!

NATALIE. But if she'd rather have you home nights—

DAVID. Natalie, *you're* a woman—Christmas will be here *soon*—would *you* rather have *Bill* home every night, or a sable stole under your tree Christmas morning ...?

NATALIE. (*after a thoughtful pause*) You've made your point.

DAVID. So do you see why I've got to keep this a secret?

NATALIE. Yes, I do.

DAVID. And—you won't *tell* Sam about it, will you–?

NATALIE. After all the trouble you've gone to, I'd be a *louse* to spill the beans! My lips are sealed.

(*They are in doorway-to-hall area now; neither of them sees SAMANTHA open bedroom door at this point and peek slightly out, curiously, toward where they stand; SAMANTHA will, of course, react appropriately to everything they now say, without revealing her presence:*)

DAVID. I really appreciate those lips of yours! They've done me a big favor!

NATALIE. What are neighbors *for?!*

DAVID. And you'll say nothing to Samantha?

NATALIE. *This* is the kind of secret every husband *should* keep from his wife!

DAVID. Of course, on Christmas morning, I fully intend to tell her about *your* part in this affair! Sam ought to learn what kind of friend you really are!

NATALIE. I'd love to see the look on her face when you spring the surprise!

DAVID. Heck, why don't you come *over* Christmas morning?! And bring Bill along!

NATALIE. Oh, definitely! Maybe our little secret will start giving *him* ideas! (*BOTH laugh*)

DAVID. Well, better get a move on!

NATALIE. I'll bet your lap is longing for a tenant by now! With a lot of greedy requests!

DAVID. *Ssssh!* Sam might hear you! Come on, let's get out of here!

(*They exit; SAMANTHA now comes fully out of bedroom, her face puckered with dismay and unhappiness; she stands center, lower lip trembling, then jerks her head for one last look toward the front door, and this bobbles the tassel-pompon on her cap past her face, she reacts to it, yanks the cap from her head, slams it onto the floor, then does a little dance on it with both feet in frustrated fury; at this moment, front door opens slightly and DAVID leans his head in, frowning in uncertainty; then he loses uncertainty and:*)

DAVID. Hey! You *are* wearing pajamas! I only just realized.

SAMANTHA. How *sweet* of you to even *notice!* *(hastily grabs up cap and replaces it on her head, angrily, on:)*

DAVID. But it's not even past dinner time yet.

SAMANTHA. I got *sleepy! Okay?!*

DAVID. *(easing from view)* Okay-okay-okay. 'Night, honey. *(shuts door and is gone.)*

SAMANTHA. *(to closed door:)* "Honey?!" *(sights on ornament-etc. boxes)* And as for *you*–! *(Picks up nearest box, raises it overhead, almost dashes it to the floor, then stops)* No. Grandma's glass treetop ornament's in there. *(sighs, lowers box)* I'd better just put these things away. *(starts to stack boxes on sofa, looks around in puzzlement, then behind sofa, etc.)* That's funny—where in the world did—? ... It was here just a moment ago ...? *(looks toward front door again, frowns in puzzlement, thinks a moment; then, coming to a decision, she goes to phone and dials; waits; then gets her party, and:)* Bill? ... Samantha Tuttle ... I did? I'm sorry. But isn't it a bit *early* to be in bed? ... No-no, don't get Natalie, it's *you* I want to talk to! ... No, not on the phone. Over here ... Well, *get* dressed, then! ... She what? ... Well, of *course* she went out, you idiot, or why would I *bother* to call you! ... No, I am *not* proposing a *tryst*, you numbskull! ... Oh, look, just get over here, will you? ... Okay, get *dressed* and get over here! ... Fine ... See you then! *(hangs up phone; stands uncertainly; clasps and unclasps her hands; paces; after maybe thirty seconds, a KNOCK at door; she opens it and DR. WILLIAM WELDON, a tallish owlish man with slightly uncombed hair and heavy-rimmed eyeglasses, garbed in pajamas, slippers, and a bathrobe, steps into room slightly; she impatiently pushes him even farther into room, shuts door swiftly, leaning back against it as if to prevent further intrusion from outside; he looks her up and down, and then:)*

WILLIAM. Are you *sure* this isn't a tryst?

SAMANTHA. (*annoyed*) What do you take me for!

WILLIAM. A pretty woman in red pajamas.

SAMANTHA. Now, really, Bill—! (*takes step toward him*)

WILLIAM. (*takes backstep*) A pretty woman in red pajamas who just finished yelling at me that it was a bit *early* to be in bed!

SAMANTHA. Bill, we are *not* going to bed!

WILLIAM. Try telling that to the next person who walks *in* here!

SAMANTHA. Bill, I just want to *talk* to you. Professionally. Any harm in that?

WILLIAM. Depends what profession you have in mind.

SAMANTHA. *Yours*, of course!

WILLIAM. (*a bit coolly*) If you're waiting for me to ask you to lie on the couch, forget it!

SAMANTHA. I am *not* seeing you as a *patient!* (*shoves him so he sits abruptly on sofa*)

WILLIAM. Then—as *what?*

SAMANTHA. (*sits beside him*) A loving friend!

WILLIAM. (*stands up*) That's what I'm *afraid* of!

SAMANTHA. *Will* you sit *down?!*

WILLIAM. (*startled, sits beside her again*) All right. Let's *be* professional. How long have you felt these urges for me?

SAMANTHA. *What* urges?

WILLIAM. Well, you're *certainly* not dressed for a chummy *chat!*

SAMANTHA. Well, neither are *you!*

WILLIAM. That's only because you sounded so *urgent* on the phone! I didn't wait to dress. Maybe I should have. (*starts to stand again, but cannot because she grabs him with both arms*)

SAMANTHA. Will you *stop* imagining I have these mad *desires* about you?!

WILLIAM. (*looks at her arms embracing him; then:*) I'll try—but you're not *helping* much ...!

SAMANTHA. Oh, don't be ridiculous! (*releases him*) That was just to keep you from popping up and down!

WILLIAM. Oh. Then—this *is* just a friendly chat? Even if you're wearing red pajamas?

SAMANTHA. Yes! Now will you *forget* my pajamas?!

WILLIAM. I'll—I'll *try*. (*after a pause*) Are those silk or nylon?

SAMANTHA. (*shrugs*) Who cares! My pajamas are not the issue here.

WILLIAM. So *you* say! What do you *think* the issue is, Samantha ...?

SAMANTHA. Stop treating me like a *patient!*

WILLIAM. You *said* you wanted me to act *professional!*

SAMANTHA. Not *act* professional—*be* professional! I want to talk to you about David. And Natalie.

WILLIAM. Natalie's gone out.

SAMANTHA. Of *course* she has! That's just my *point!* *She's* gone—and *David's* gone! *Now* do you see why I asked you to come over?

WILLIAM. Absolutely! (*jumps to his feet, starts for door at a run*) I'll send you my bill!

SAMANTHA. I am *not* in love with you!

WILLIAM. (*stops with hand on doorknob, frowns; then:*) You're not?

SAMANTHA. Not even slightly.

WILLIAM. (*releases knob*) Why? What's *wrong* with me?

SAMANTHA. (*patiently*) Not a thing, Bill. You're handsome, you're charming, you're intelligent and you make lots and lots of money.

WILLIAM. But you don't love me.

SAMANTHA. But I don't love you.

WILLIAM. (*returns to where she still sits on sofa, looks down at her; then:*) Maybe you *do* need professional help!

SAMANTHA. Where should I start? This is all so difficult.

WILLIAM. Well, we've established, without a doubt, that you're not in love with me. (*sits beside her.*)

SAMANTHA. Right.—How's Natalie?

WILLIAM. Fine. (*stands*) That was easy.

SAMANTHA. (*grabs his arm and pulls him back onto sofa*) I mean *how* is Natalie?

WILLIAM. Are you trying to tell me something?

SAMANTHA. Where is Natalie right now?

WILLIAM. She said she was going shopping.

SAMANTHA. And you *believed* her?

WILLIAM. Maybe you're right. (*dryly*) Going shopping around Christmas is *very* suspicious!

SAMANTHA. Don't you think it's also very strange that *David* isn't here?

WILLIAM. (*putting her on*) Do you think that—maybe *he's* out shopping too? And at Christmas!

SAMANTHA. No, David says he's at work. But, you know what I found before David came home?

WILLIAM. What? A charge card? A Christmas list? Oh, what a tangled web!

SAMANTHA. Will you stop that? I'm serious. I found a—Santa outfit!

WILLIAM. (*holding back the laughter*) And, at Christmas time. Some people!

SAMANTHA. But it disappeared. Don't you think that's strange?

WILLIAM. (*finally laughing out loud*) Maybe David's the Santa burglar.

SAMANTHA. (*stands*) I thought you were my friend. You wouldn't be laughing if you heard the conversation *I* heard between David and Natalie. They were discussing their sordid little affair!

WILLIAM. David and Natalie? (*stands*) Wait a minute. You think—

SAMANTHA. If I hadn't heard it with my own ears I wouldn't have believed it myself. I heard them discussing how much she *wanted* to be sitting on his lap.

WILLIAM. Samantha, are you sure? Couldn't it just be your imagination?

SAMANTHA. Bill, I know what I heard. (*crosses to tree*) They're planning on telling us Christmas morning. I can hear them now! "Merry Christmas, Bill and Samantha! We're dumping you and running away to Bora Bora!"

WILLIAM. They *said* Bora Bora?

SAMANTHA. No, but that's where lovers run *off* to.

WILLIAM. Not in this case. (*is putting her on*) I would think they would choose a much colder place. (*crosses to her*) It adds up. A Santa Claus outfit. And a lap! This is terrible! If what you're telling me is the truth, they definitely need professional help. It's a sad, sad case. You'd better sit down.

SAMANTHA. (*sits at sofa, worriedly attentive*) Sounds like you're familiar with cases like these.

WILLIAM. (*still not taking SAMANTHA seriously; sits on arm of sofa next to her*) What we have here is what is known as the *North Pole Syndrome*. It's very rare but happens this time of year. Two friends, in this case David and Natalie, have a romantic fantasy. He dresses as Santa Claus, and she dresses as Santa's little helper.

SAMANTHA. I *knew* it! What can we do?

WILLIAM. (*stands and crosses to left behind sofa*) We've got to act fast before it's too late. We can only hope we've caught it in the early stages. In the final stages it's

not a pretty sight! The two of them will think it's
Christmas year 'round. They'll be addicted to Bing Crosby
movies and Christmas carols. They'll eat nothing but
fruitcake and eggnog. They'll go through all their life
savings buying presents and decorating any evergreen tree
they see. In a worst-case scenario, they'll resort to stealing
reindeer and trying to fly off of tall buildings.

SAMANTHA. *(with great concern)* And then—?

WILLIAM. *(with mock sincerity)* You'll see reindeer
and the poor souls embedded in the sidewalk somewhere—
still smiling. *(trying hard to keep back the laughter)* It's
tragic!

SAMANTHA. *(stands)* Can anything be done? We've
got to do something! *(crosses to him; then: suddenly
realizes that WILLIAM has been joking with her)* Bill! So
you think it's funny! There is no such thing as North Pole
Syndrome, is there?

WILLIAM. Of course not, Samantha! *(puts arm around
her)* Your accusations about Natalie and David are just as
silly. Why would David *do* anything like *that* when he's
got such a beautiful and loving wife? And, of course,
Natalie's got *me!* You just have a very active imagination.
I'm sure there's a very *logical* explanation for what you
heard. I wouldn't worry about it.

SAMANTHA. I guess you're right. I think I'm going
to call David at his office and apologize to him for even
thinking him guilty.

WILLIAM. There you go! What a good idea. While
you're doing that I'm going back over and wait for the
damage report when Natalie gets back from shopping. Why
does Neiman-Marcus have to have a charge card? I think we
could wipe out the total indebtedness of Brazil with what
Natalie charges on that card!

SAMANTHA. Well, why don't you just close the
account?

WILLIAM. And miss out on the fun of the guilt trip I can put on her? That charge receipt is material for several weeks of good old-fashioned blackmail. She feels so guilty, I can get away with almost *anything* for at *least* two months!

SAMANTHA. That's dishonest—using her like that. You ought to be ashamed.

WILLIAM. Oh, I am—for about ten seconds. (*exits*)

SAMANTHA. (*closes door, chuckling to herself*) How could I ever suspect David? (*crosses to phone; then as she dials:*) David, you're not going to believe what I was thinking. I thought that you and Natalie were—Hello.— May I speak to David Tuttle, please?—He's not there? This is his desk, isn't it?—You don't know. Well, who is this?—You're Ralph, the maintenance engineer? Can you ask someone else if they know where Mr. Tuttle is?— You're the only one in that area. The office has been closed since five? (*suddenly concerned*) There must be some mistake.—The office *always* closes at five ... especially during the *holiday* season?—No. No message. (*hangs up; then to herself:*) I'm sure there's a logical explanation. (*there's a KNOCK at the door; crosses to door*) Who's there?

WILLIAM. (*offstage*) It's me, Bill. I locked myself out.

SAMANTHA. (*opens door*) I'm so glad you came back. It's awful. (*as he enters she runs to him and gives him a big embrace*)

WILLIAM. (*off-guard*) This isn't the first time I've locked myself out.

SAMANTHA. (*in tears*) Bill, you're such a good friend.

WILLIAM. You're a good friend, too, Samantha. (*they are standing in front of door when they hear offstage voice of NATALIE; BOTH react:*)

NATALIE. Samantha? (*KNOCK at door; WILLIAM, nearest door, instinctively gets behind SAMANTHA*)

WILLIAM. It's Natalie!

SAMANTHA. (*reaching for doorknob, angrily*) I want a *word* with her!

WILLIAM. (*spins her to face him*) *I* don't! Not in *this* outfit!

SAMANTHA. (*struggling to get out of his grasp*) But *we're* not having an affair!

WILLIAM. No, but we're sure *dressed* for it!

NATALIE. (*KNOCKS again*) Samantha, are you *in* there—?! (*she starts to open door; WILLIAM takes a terrified backstep, still clutching SAMANTHA, arm of sofa catches him at back of knees, and he topples over arm onto sofa, with SAMANTHA lying prone on top of him [their faces are cheek-to-cheek so that BOTH are facing out front, wide-eyed with fright]; NATALIE steps in, purse slung over one wrist, both arms holding small stack of gift-wrapped packages; from her viewpoint, she can see two pairs of feet over sofa-arm, no faces*) Samantha, I wonder if you could be a dear, and—(*reacts to feet*) Oh! I thought you said David *wasn't* home!

SAMANTHA. (*desperately*) He came back!

NATALIE. Do you know—*Bill* has pajamas just *like* those!

SAMANTHA. (*a hollow laugh*) Men! They're all alike!

NATALIE. (*starts around to front of sofa*) Did I come at a bad time? (*WILLIAM grabs Santa cap off SAMANTHA's head, dons it himself, pulling it down completely over his face*)

SAMANTHA. (*despite amorous tableau*) What makes you say *that?*

NATALIE. Well, it looks as if all your romantic problems have been *solved!*

SAMANTHA. That'd be *my* guess!

NATALIE. Do you know—Bill has a *robe* just like that, *too!*

SAMANTHA. *Does* he, now!

NATALIE. I feel so sorry for men! Women have a *much* larger selection when it comes to clothing!

SAMANTHA. Natalie, if it hasn't crossed your mind yet—we *are* just a bit—uh—busy ...!

NATALIE. (*reacts*) *Oh!* (*starts backing doorward*) Oh, dear, what was I *thinking* of! Of *course* you are! I was just so pleased to discover your troubles are *over* that I—!

SAMANTHA. We under*stand!* Nice seeing you! Happy holidays!

NATALIE. (*in doorway, pauses*) Oh, but I forgot to tell you *why* I stopped by!

SAMANTHA. I forgive you! 'Bye, now!

NATALIE. But you see—I just bought this present for Bill, and I wondered if I could hide it in *your* apartment till Christmas morning?

SAMANTHA. Just leave it by the door!

NATALIE. Can't I put it under the tree?

SAMANTHA. All right! Yes! Anything! But hurry!

NATALIE. (*starting toward tree*) I'm moving as fast as I can!

SAMANTHA. I'm sorry to rush you—but David's romantic moods don't last very long!

NATALIE. Of course! (*sets largest of wrapped packages under tree, heads doorward with rest*) I sure wish *Bill* would get amorous early in the evening!

SAMANTHA. (*with a glance at man beneath her*) *This* evening?

NATALIE. *Any* evening! Ah, well! I'm certainly *envious* of you two!

SAMANTHA. Good*bye*, Natalie!

NATALIE. (*missing urgency*) Ta-ta, Samantha. (*hand on knob, ready to exit*) 'Bye, David! ... David?

SAMANTHA. David *never* talks when he's feeling romantic!

NATALIE. Whyever not?

SAMANTHA. It breaks the mood! *Please* don't break David's mood!

NATALIE. Oh, of course not! Sorry! See you later! (*exits, shutting door*)

WILLIAM. (*as he and SAMANTHA scramble swiftly apart and lurch to their feet*) Is she gone?

SAMANTHA. (*pulls cap from his face*) Look for yourself! (*puts cap on own head again*)

WILLIAM. Wow, *that* was a close one!

SAMANTHA. You're telling *me*! You'd better get *out* of here, quick, before she comes back!

WILLIAM. (*takes step doorward, stops*) I can't go back to our apartment dressed like *this*!

SAMANTHA. Well, you certainly can't stay *here*!

WILLIAM. But how can I *explain* this outfit to Natalie?

SAMANTHA. Can't you listen at your apartment door till she's in the kitchen, or something, and then *sneak* in?

WILLIAM. I haven't got my *key*, remember?!

SAMANTHA. Oh, damn.

WILLIAM. What am I going to do?!

SAMANTHA. (*thinks a second; then:*) *I've* got it! Put on one of *David's* suits and go home in that!

WILLIAM. But Natalie *knows* all my suits!

SAMANTHA. Tell her you bought yourself a *new* one! (*starts pushing him toward bedroom door*)

WILLIAM. (*resisting*) But then I'll have to *keep* the suit!

SAMANTHA. You can pay me for it later! (*pushing again*)

WILLIAM. (*resisting again*) But what'll you tell *David* when he can't *find* his suit?

SAMANTHA. He'll never miss it! He's an executive. All his suits look alike.

WILLIAM. But, Samantha—!

SAMANTHA. Will you get *in* there?! (*shoves him through bedroom door, pulls it closed*)

WILLIAM. (*off*) Where's the light switch? I can't see a thing!

SAMANTHA. (*not seeing NATALIE once again peeking in at front door*) There's a lamp on my dressing table! Walk straight forward, *carefully*, and grope at about belt-height! (*listens; there is a pause—then a CRASH offstage*)

WILLIAM. *Aaaaah!* (*a cry of pain*)

NATALIE. (*steps into room, concerned*) What happened?! (*She still carries other packages*)

SAMANTHA. (*whirls, sees her*) Natalie!

NATALIE. Did David hurt himself? I heard a scream!

SAMANTHA. No-no! That was just a growl of—of *passion!* He gets like that.

NATALIE. Then what are *you* doing out *here?*

SAMANTHA. He *scares* me when he gets this passionate!

NATALIE. (*ruefully*) Some wives have all the luck!

SAMANTHA. Natalie, for heaven's sake, what are you *doing* here again?!

NATALIE. (*heads treeward*) I left the wrong package!

SAMANTHA. Well, *make* your swap, and then please—if you don't mind—get *out* of here!

NATALIE. (*switching one package for another*) I will, I will, I will! You don't have to get *growly!*

SAMANTHA. Every moment you're here, David's likely to *change* his *mood!* Wouldn't *you* get growly?

NATALIE. (*heading doorward with proper packages*) I'm going, I'm going! (*but, at door, stops*) Wait a minute—if you're *scared* of the way he's acting, don't you *want* his mood to change?

SAMANTHA. (*shrugs inanely*) Part of me says yes—
part of me says no—you know how silly *love* gets!

NATALIE. Maybe I should stick around till you're
sure—?!

SAMANTHA. Damn it, I'm *sure*, I'm *sure!*

NATALIE. So why aren't you going into the bedroom,
then?

SAMANTHA. All right, I'll go! (*opens door [there is
LIGHT from bedroom, now], looks inside, then gives a
SCREAM at what she sees—and we hear WILLIAM give
another SCREAM of his own—and then she quickly closes
door and leans back against it*)

NATALIE. What's the matter?

SAMANTHA. He's—not quite *dressed* yet!

NATALIE. But—considering his *mood*—why do you
want him dressed?!

SAMANTHA. (*has had it; starts for NATALIE,
dangerously*) Listen, Nat, *you* do romance *your* way, and
we'll do it *our* way! *Okay?!*

NATALIE. (*backing out door*) Okay-Okay! Sorry I
asked!

SAMANTHA. (*shuts door, hard; leans back against it,
gasping*) I'm too *old* for this kind of thing!

WILLIAM. (*entering from bedroom*) How do I look—?
(*and he's wearing blue pants, a brown jacket, one black
shoe and one brown shoe*)

SAMANTHA. *Fine*, if you're determined to *blow* your
marriage! Bill, nothing on you *matches!*

WILLIAM. (*looks down*) Oh, damn! I got dressed so
fast that— (*then BOTH react as front door starts to open;
WILLIAM leaps for cover, ending up flat on floor in front
of sofa, shielded from view of anyone at door, as DAVID
comes in, with a large plastic [garbage-type] bag [in which
his Santa suit is hidden]; he reacts to SAMANTHA, whips
bag behind back, backsteps into hall door, which closes*)

DAVID. Sam! You're still up!

SAMANTHA. (*acutely aware of WILLIAM's presence*) David! You're home!

DAVID. I thought you'd be *glad*—?

SAMANTHA. Oh, I *am*, I *am*! Hey—let's go *out*!

DAVID. *Out*?! But—you're not *dressed*!

SAMANTHA. Let's go out anyway! (*KNOCK at front door*)

NATALIE. (*off*) Samantha—? Yoo-hoo—?!

SAMANTHA. Oh, *no*! (*springs into his arms*) Darling—quick—act like you're mad with desire!

DAVID. (*arms behind her back, flings bag from view in front of sofa [onto WILLIAM]* Now?!

SAMANTHA. No time like the present! (*kisses him fiercely; as he happily responds, NATALIE peeks in*)

NATALIE. Sorry, you guys, this *other* present is for Bill, too!

SAMANTHA. (*breaks kiss briefly*) Under the tree, then *out* of here!

NATALIE. Gotcha! (*dashes to put single present with other one, hurries back toward front door, on:*) My, David, but you're a quick dresser!

DAVID. (*breaks from kiss*) I'm a *what*—?

SAMANTHA. A mad, passionate beast! (*kisses him even more fiercely*)

NATALIE. (*pausing on threshold*) Sometime, Samantha, I wish you'd tell me what you *feed* this guy!

DAVID. (*breaks happily from kiss*) I wish I knew what *she's* been feeding on!

SAMANTHA. I live for love! (*kisses him again*)

NATALIE. I'd better go! (*exits during:*)

DAVID. (*breaking from kiss*) Yes, and hurry! (*as NATALIE closes door and is gone, he starts to zero in for another kiss, but now SAMANTHA pushes him angrily away*)

SAMANTHA. Don't you *dare* try to kiss me, you beast!

DAVID. I thought you *liked* me passionate?!

SAMANTHA. I mean a *different* kind of beast! Where *were* you tonight?!

DAVID. I *told* you—I had to go to the office and—

SAMANTHA. I tried to *phone* you there!

DAVID. (*instantly, almost without pause from preceding line of his:*)—the office was *closed!* So I came home.

SAMANTHA. David, you and I are going to have a long, long *talk,* and right this minute! (*has started around to front of sofa—belatedly remembers WILLIAM as she sees him there, reacts with terror, instantly whirls to stop DAVID's move in that direction, grabs him in her arms madly*) But first—let's get *out* of here! We need a long walk *and* a long talk. You start without me.

DAVID. (*confused*) We're going to talk—but I'm supposed to start *without* you?

SAMANTHA. The *walk*—not the talk. I need to—organize my thoughts briefly. So, take your coat and wait for me out front, *downstairs,* and I'll get my coat, get my thoughts together, and meet you out front. (*gets coat and tosses it to DAVID*) Now, I'll be there shortly. (*reluctantly, DAVID exits. She then rushes over to WILLIAM. Then: with panic*) Bill, you've got to help me. I called David's office and it was closed.

WILLIAM. (*slowly standing up*) David just told you the same thing.

SAMANTHA. But, the janitor at his office said the office has been closing at five *every night* during the holiday season! Where has David *been?*

WILLIAM. I have no idea. There's got to be a logical—

SAMANTHA. He's been with another *woman!* I know it! I can *feel* it! Bill, are you going to help me or not? I want to save my marriage!

WILLIAM. Samantha, you're jumping to conclusions.

SAMANTHA. Bill, are you going to help me or not? (*before he can answer*) Don't forget, the *other woman* could be *Natalie!*

WILLIAM. Are you going to start *that* again?

SAMANTHA. (*takes him by the arm and sits him on sofa. Sits next to him*) Remember the conversation I heard?

WILLIAM. Okay, if David was with Natalie, then why was she here without him and him without her? And when they saw each other they weren't surprised!

SAMANTHA. Well—I don't know! Maybe that was just to throw us off the track. But, I have a plan. *Hypnotize* David into loving me again. And then you can get Natalie back.

WILLIAM. (*stands*) I don't *want* her back! I *mean*, I don't think I need to *get* her back—What I'm *trying* to say is that I don't think David and Natalie *are* having a fling. As a matter of fact, I don't think *David is flinging* with *anyone!*

SAMANTHA. (*stands*) So, why *not* hypnotize David? If he's not having a fling with anyone, then he'll still love me—but if he's flinging, then you can have Natalie back—or, if he's not flinging with Natalie you can have her back anyway. What would it hurt?

WILLIAM. Hypnosis is *not* something that should be used indiscriminately. It's not some parlor game or nightclub entertainment. It is a clinical technique which should not be used except in very special, controlled situations.

SAMANTHA. Isn't saving the marriage of your best friends very special? What could it hurt?

WILLIAM. (*considering*) Well—

SAMANTHA. *Please?*

WILLIAM. Fine! Like you said, what *harm* could come from hypnotizing David into loving *you?* I *still* think that's redundant! But, as a personal favor, I'll hypnotize David for you! Okay?

SAMANTHA. (*gives him a big hug*) You're wonderful, Bill.

WILLIAM. Haven't we been though this before? (*she un-hugs*) So *when* do you want me to hypnotize him?

SAMANTHA. As soon as possible. I tell you what— you get ready whatever paraphernalia you need while I go downstairs and talk to David. Then I'll make some excuse to send him back up here. Then you can hypnotize him. Then I'll come back and David and I—and you and Natalie—can *all* live happily ever after!

WILLIAM. Hypnotism doesn't come cheap. (*pauses as she reacts, then smiles*) Will you relax? I *did* say personal *favor!* Now, get *out* of here while I get ready to control your husband's *mind!*

SAMANTHA. You're a doll. (*grabs her topcoat, exits to hall, closing door after her, during his line:*)

WILLIAM. I hope my colleagues don't find out about this. They wouldn't take kindly to my hypnotizing one person into loving someone else—especially for *free!* (*SAMANTHA, just in doorway, now laughs, gives him a wave, and completes her exit. Alone, he continues in a mumble:*) Now, let's see—I need a focal-object ... (*exits into bedroom*)

(*A pause. Then there is a shaking of the door knob. Suddenly the door is slowly opened, and KRIS KREIGLE, a burglar, dressed in a Santa outfit, including hat and beard, cautiously enters the room. He looks and walks around, then he tiptoes to the telephone, dials, and then, on phone:*)

KRIS. Sheila? ... Kris ... Yeah, everything's going just fine. I'm at the final apartment right now, you know where it's at? ... Good. Bring the car around front in about ten minutes ... Naw, no problem. I'll pick up what I can, then be out of here fast ... See you in about ten minutes, honey ... Merry Christmas! (*hangs up phone, brings out plastic bag, identical to the one DAVID is carrying his costume in, from inside jacket, tiptoes offstage into kitchen. Then WILLIAM enters from bedroom, still empty-handed, and still mismatched of clothing; he looks about, frowning, then sights on ornament-box near tree, hurries over and lifts out sparkling ornament from box, dangling from its hook, holds it up to light, nods and—*)

WILLIAM. Perfect! (*then he reacts as KRIS comes out of kitchen, the bag now containing something heavy which clinks a lot [the silverware, of course]; KRIS sees him and freezes*) David, why are you dressed in that Santa suit?

KRIS. (*in deep Santa-like voice*) What's wrong with this outfit? It looks a heck of a lot better than *yours!*

WILLIAM. Mine? (*looks down at himself, reacts*) Oh, damn! I can *explain!*

KRIS. But why *should* you?

WILLIAM. Wait, maybe I won't *have* to! (*deep, soothing voice:*) Look! Look into the pretty ornament, David! (*dangles it before KRIS's eyes*)

KRIS. Cute as hell. Well, if you'll excuse me—(*tries to move toward hall door*)

WILLIAM. Where are you going? Didn't Sam tell you to come up here and *stay?*

KRIS. Who's Sam?

WILLIAM. Oh, David, this is worse than I even suspected! Denial of even *knowing* the woman you love above all others! I'd better take action fast! Sit down on the sofa.

KRIS. Why should I?

WILLIAM. You surely don't expect me to let you *leave* here, do you?

KRIS. I guess it *was* a forlorn hope. (*shuffles to sofa*) I suppose now you're going to call the *cops?*

WILLIAM. Why would I do *that?* Now sit. (*pushes KRIS down*) What are friends for? No one has to know about this.

KRIS. (*confused*) They don't?

WILLIAM. (*sits beside KRIS*) Why should we tell anybody about this? It'll be a secret between *you ... Sam ...* and *me!*

KRIS. Fair enough! (*tries to stand*) I really have to go now.

WILLIAM. (*pulls him back onto sofa*) I'm not *through* with you yet!

KRIS. You're not?

WILLIAM. (*sits on sofa facing KRIS, dangles ornament before his eyes*) I want you to take a close look at this bauble! I want you to watch it—carefully. (*begins to move ornament from side to side; KRIS follows motion with eyes and head*)

KRIS. Carefully.

WILLIAM. Side to side.

KRIS. Side to side.

WILLIAM. You are getting sleepy—sleepy.

KRIS. (*sleepily*) Sleepy. (*closes eyes*)

WILLIAM. Relax. Listen only to my voice.

KRIS. Only to your voice.

WILLIAM. Now, open your eyes slowly. (*KRIS opens his eyes. He is in a trance. WILLIAM puts ornament aside*) I want you to listen to my voice and follow my directions. You are in love with Samantha. Only Samantha.

KRIS. (*trancelike*) Samantha who?

WILLIAM. Samantha Tuttle, your loving wife.

KRIS. My loving wife.

WILLIAM. You love only her.

KRIS. I love only her. (*pause; then:*) Why?

WILLIAM. Because you are her husband, *David* Tuttle, of course!

KRIS. I am *David* Tuttle, of course.

WILLIAM. You are not interested in any other woman.

KRIS. I am not interested in any other woman.

WILLIAM. As soon as you see Samantha you will kiss her passionately like you've never kissed her before.

KRIS. I will kiss her passionately like I've never kissed her before.

WILLIAM. There was something else.

KRIS. There was something else.

WILLIAM. (*reacts briefly. Then remembers and looks at suit*) Oh, yes, you will *not* remember that I am wearing your clothes!

KRIS. I will *not* remember that you are wearing my clothes!

WILLIAM. I want you to close your eyes. (*KRIS does.*) Now when I snap my fingers you will follow the directions I have given, but you will not be consciously aware of them. They will be all in your subconscious. (*snaps fingers. KRIS opens eyes*)

KRIS. I think I need to go now. I've got to find— Samantha. (*stands*)

(*Suddenly door opens and DAVID and SAMANTHA enter.
    WILLIAM gapes in surprise*)

WILLIAM. *David?! Samantha?!*

KRIS. Samantha! (*rushes to her*) I love you! (*grabs SAMANTHA in embrace and kisses her passionately. SAMANTHA, being caught off guard has had no time to fight the embrace*)

WILLIAM. What the hell? (*stands with jaw hanging open*)

DAVID. Why are you kissing my wife?!

KRIS. (*breaks from kiss, points to WILLIAM*) He *told* me to!

DAVID. (*to WILLIAM*) You *told* this clown to kiss my wife?!

WILLIAM. (*defensively*) It wasn't *my* idea, it was *Sam's!*

DAVID. Sam! You told Bill to *tell* this guy to kiss you?!

SAMANTHA. Not exactly ...

DAVID. Not *exactly?!*

SAMANTHA. Actually—I've never seen this Santa before in my life!

KRIS. Is that any way to talk about your husband?!

DAVID. Samantha—you married Santa Claus?!

SAMANTHA. Why *would* I? I can scarcely survive with *one* husband!

KRIS. (*abruptly sweeps her up into his arms*) Samantha, I love you more than any other woman in the world! (*starts toting her toward bedroom*)

DAVID. Who *says* so?!

KRIS. (*nodding toward WILLIAM in passing*) He does!

DAVID. (*squaring off for a fist fight with WILLIAM*) *You* does?!

WILLIAM. No, I doesn't! I mean—it was an honest mistake!

KRIS. (*to SAMANTHA, nearly at bedroom door*) I love you, I love you, I love you!

SAMANTHA. (*screaming in terror*) David, aren't you going to *help* me?!

KRIS. I *am* helping you! That's what husbands are *for!*

DAVID. *He's* David, too?

WILLIAM. That's what I *told* him!

DAVID. *WHY?!*

KRIS. (*still trance-like*) It was an honest mistake. (*exits into bedroom with SAMANTHA*)

DAVID. Hey, *wait* a minute—! (*rushes to bedroom door just as it closes, and can't open it*) He's locked us out!

WILLIAM. Can you blame him?

DAVID. (*pounds on door*) Samantha!

SAMANTHA. (*off*) Helllllp!

DAVID. (*to WILLIAM*) We've got to break the door down!

NATALIE. (*enters from hall, carrying the bag that DAVID had earlier*) What's all the *screaming* in here?!

WILLIAM. (*points wearily toward DAVID who is manfully trying to break down door without the least bit of success*) He saw Sammy kissing *Santa Claus!*

(*And as SAMANTHA, in bedroom, gives final wordless scream of terror—*)

THE CURTAIN FALLS

End of Act I

ACT II

SCENE: The same. Two-and-a-half seconds later. WILLIAM, DAVID and NATALIE where we left them before. We hear SAMANTHA, off, give another scream of terror. Then:)

NATALIE. Bill! Run to our apartment and get help!

WILLIAM. Right! (*gallops out into hall*)

DAVID. Who's *in* your apartment?

NATALIE. (*rushes to him*) Nobody! I didn't want Bill to see me give you *this!* (*thrusts bag into his hands*) Why did you leave it outside my door?

DAVID. I couldn't very well let Sam see me bring it in *here!* Say—how did you know *I* left it?

NATALIE. Who *else* has a Santa suit around here?!

SAMANTHA. (*off*) Hellllp!

DAVID. (*points to bedroom*) He does!

NATALIE. *Who?* Who's *in* there with Sam?

DAVID. Some clown in a Santa suit!

NATALIE. The Santa burglar!

DAVID. Do you really think so?!

SAMANTHA. (*off*) David! *David! DAVID!*

KRIS. (*off*) Yes, darling?

NATALIE. (*indicates bag*) Why is your Santa suit soaking wet?

DAVID. Some stupid *elf* was smoking in the locker room at the store and set the *sprinklers* off! That's why I'm home early. Couldn't work in a soggy suit, could I? My beard looks like a drowned rabbit!

WILLIAM. (*rushing back into room*) Get help from *who?* There's *no* one *in* our apartment!

39

NATALIE. Then try *another* apartment!

WILLIAM. Right! (*gallops out again*)

SAMANTHA. (*off*) Let me go! Let me go! Stop, you're tickling me! (*starts hysterical laughter*)

DAVID. Natalie, how are you at breaking down doors?

NATALIE. Don't you have a key to the door?

DAVID. Hey, I forgot about that! There's a little gizmo like a screwdriver fits into the knob!

NATALIE. So *use* it!

DAVID. I don't know where Sam *keeps* it! (*pounds on bedroom door*) Sam! Where's the little *gizmo?!*

SAMANTHA. (*off*) Chasing me around the bed!

DAVID. I mean the bedroom-doorknob-key gizmo!

SAMANTHA. (*off*) At the back of the kitchen drawer, behind the silverware!

DAVID. Right! (*gallops off into kitchen*)

WILLIAM. (*gallops in from hall*) There's nobody home!

NATALIE. Where?

WILLIAM. *Anywhere!*

NATALIE. Are you sure?

WILLIAM. How *can* there be anyone else home in this building? They'd have been at the door complaining about all this racket!

NATALIE. Say, where did you get that *suit?* And those *shoes?*

WILLIAM. Uh ... They were on sale!

DAVID. (*galloping in from kitchen*) The silverware's gone!

NATALIE. Never mind the silverware, where's the little gizmo?!

WILLIAM. What little gizmo?

DAVID. The one that unlocks the— (*pauses, looks at him closely*) Funny, *I* have a suit like that one—except the *pants* match.

NATALIE. How about the shoes?

DAVID. Them too.

SAMANTHA. (*off*) Hellllp!

KRIS. (*off*) I love you, I love you, I love you!

SAMANTHA. (*off*) Well, *I* don't love *you!*

KRIS. (*off*) Then why are you wearing those sexy pajamas?!

SAMANTHA. (*off*) Hellllp!

NATALIE. She should *never* have worn those pajamas!

DAVID. Why *did* she?

NATALIE. To make *you* stay home from the *office!*

WILLIAM. No *wonder* the guy can't stay away from her! She looks *gorgeous* in them!

DAVID. (*inspired*) Of course! That's the problem! (*shouts through bedroom door:*) Samantha, take off those pajamas!

SAMANTHA. (*off*) Whaaat?!

DAVID. (*to OTHERS*) Bad idea?

NATALIE/WILLIAM. (*nodding solemnly*) Bad idea.

KRIS. (*off*) I love you, I love you, I love you!

SAMANTHA. (*off*) Well, *I* don't love *you!* (*bedroom door flies open and SAMANTHA gallops out, running downstage of sofa, with KRIS in amorous pursuit; DAVID, NATALIE and WILLIAM chase after him, till the fivesome are running in a circle around the sofa, during:*)

DAVID. There he goes!

NATALIE. Stop him!

WILLIAM. He sure can run for a little guy!

SAMANTHA. Help me! Help me!

KRIS. I love you, I love you, I love you!

SAMANTHA. Bill, can't you *un*hypnotize him?!

NATALIE. Bill! Have you been hypnotizing people *again?*

SAMANTHA. "Again?!"

DAVID. What the hell goes *on* in this place when I'm away at work?!

SAMANTHA. *Ha!* Don't give me that! I *know* you weren't at work tonight!

NATALIE. Of course not—he's *home!*

WILLIAM. (*tiring of the circular pursuit*) Hey, *I've* got an idea! (*ALL halt*)

OTHERS. What?

WILLIAM. Let's run the *other* way! (*ALL immediately reverse, so that now KRIS is chasing WILLIAM, WILLIAM is chasing NATALIE, NATALIE is chasing DAVID, and DAVID is chasing SAMANTHA, during:*)

SAMANTHA. Don't run *away* from him, Bill—hypnotize him!

WILLIAM. (*as WILLIAM continues, ALL FIVE runners slow little-by-little until ALL are moving like the slow-motion runners in a dream, during:*) Your eyelids are getting heavy, *oh*-so-heavy ... you can hear nothing but the sound of my voice ... I am going to count backwards from five, and when I reach zero, you will be asleep ... five ... four ... three ... two ... one ... *zero!* (*ALL but WILLIAM sag gently to the floor, eyes closed, smiling happily; he stares in confusion, then belatedly reacts*) Oops, I overdid it!

SHEILA. (*appears in still-open hall doorway*) Kris! What have they done to you?!

WILLIAM. Who the hell are you?

SHEILA. (*producing pistol from purse*) None of your business! Stick 'em up!

WILLIAM. (*raising hands*) That seems fair enough.

SHEILA. (*shuts door behind her, rushes to KRIS, still keeping pistol pointed at WILLIAM*) What's the matter with him? What have you *done* to him?

WILLIAM. He's just asleep! Honest!

SHEILA. (*shaking KRIS*) So why doesn't he wake up?

WILLIAM. He can't until I tell him to!

SHEILA. So *tell* him to!

WILLIAM. Wake up! *Please* wake up! (*KRIS—and OTHERS, of course—abruptly come to their feet*)

SHEILA. Kris, are you all right?

SAMANTHA. Who's *she?*

NATALIE. What's going on?

DAVID. Why is she pointing that pistol?

KRIS. Who's *Kris?*

SHEILA. I thought *you* were! (*pulls away his beard*) And you *are!*

KRIS. Keep your distance, lady!

SHEILA. Kris, are you nuts?! Come on, we've got to get *out* of here! (*grabs his arm*)

KRIS. (*pulls free*) Lady, who *are* you?!

SHEILA. I'm *Sheila!* Honey, don't you *know* me? When you didn't come down to the *car* after ten minutes, I got panicky and came up here to *help* you!

KRIS. What car? Why are you calling me "honey"?

SAMANTHA. (*to DAVID*) Oh, David, I was so scared—! (*embraces him*)

KRIS. You take your hands off my wife!

SHEILA. Your *wife?!* She *can't* be your wife!

NATALIE. Why not?!

SHEILA. Because *I'm* his *fiancee!*

KRIS. (*embracing SAMANTHA, even if she's in DAVID's embrace, too*) It's a lie!

SHEILA. Who's that woman you're hugging?

KRIS. Samantha Tuttle, the only woman I will ever love!

NATALIE. (*to WILLIAM*) William Weldon, what have you *done?!*

WILLIAM. I might ask *you* the same *question!*

SAMANTHA. He was just trying to save my marriage, Natalie!

DAVID. By giving you another *husband?*

SHEILA. *Husband?* Kris, what's he talking about?

KRIS. Stop calling me "Kris!" My name is David Tuttle!

DAVID. Impossible! *My* name is David Tuttle!

SHEILA. *Exclusively?*

DAVID. Uh—well, *no*, but—

NATALIE. Bill, will you get him *out* of your magic spell before Sheila *shoots* us all?!

WILLIAM. I'll try! (*to SHEILA*) With your permission, of course—?

SHEILA. Yes, yes, *anything!*

WILLIAM. You can *still* hear only *my* voice, David! Your real name is— (*to SHEILA*) What *is* his real name?

SAMANTHA. "Kris Kreigle!"

WILLIAM. Your real name is "Kris Kreigle," and when I snap my fingers you will awaken and no longer think you are David Tuttle! You *do not* love Samantha! You love—

SHEILA. Sheila!

WILLIAM. Sheila! (*snaps fingers*) There!

DAVID. (*rushing into SHEILA's arms*) Darling! You came *back* to me!

SAMANTHA. Oh, great, now *he's* got a new identity!

WILLIAM. *Oops!*

SHEILA. I want *my* Kris back!

DAVID. You got him, babe! (*tries to smother SHEILA with kisses and hugs. She drops gun to floor.*)

SHEILA. Wait a minute! (*takes off running toward kitchen with DAVID chasing her. KRIS starts looking longingly at SAMANTHA*)

SAMANTHA. Don't you start that again! (*she takes off running with KRIS chasing after her. They loop around the sofa and head out front door*)

NATALIE. You've *really* done it this time! (*during the chase ad-libs from group such as "I love you," "help," screams, etc. SHEILA and DAVID run out of kitchen as SAMANTHA and KRIS run in from front door. They all begin looping around sofa. One group runs clockwise, the other runs counter-clockwise. After a couple of laps the men switch chasing ladies. After two laps they realize that they have switched and resume chasing their original prey)* This is like watching a figure-eight stock car race.

SHEILA. *Help! (she heads out front door with DAVID hot on her heels)*

SAMANTHA. *Bill! (she heads out front door with KRIS hot on her heels)*

NATALIE. Bill, what on earth have you done? You told me hypnosis should *only* be used in a controlled clinical situation!

WILLIAM. *(shrugs)* Well, this proves I was right!

NATALIE. *(crosses to door)* Shouldn't we go *after* them?

WILLIAM. They'll be back.

NATALIE. What makes you so sure?

WILLIAM. This is their *home!* But while we're waiting—What have you and *David* been up to? There's something strange going on here, and I *demand* to know what it *is!*

NATALIE. *You* hypnotize David and this Kris character into chasing each other's women, and *I'm* supposed to explain the strange goings-on?

WILLIAM. I mean the *other* strange thing going on! Between you and David! Samantha overheard you two planning a Christmas *surprise! What* surprise?!

NATALIE. *(hedging)* If I *told* you, it wouldn't *be* a surprise! *(sees gun and picks it up)* Right? *(points it at him for emphasis)*

WILLIAM. *Don't shoot!* I don't *need* to know about the surprise!

NATALIE. Bill, what's gotten *into* you? *I* just picked up the gun so no one would *trip* over it!

WILLIAM. You're not going to *shoot* me?

NATALIE. (*snidely*) What, and spoil the *surprise?* (*crosses to door with gun still in hand*) Oh-oh! You'd better look out. Here they come! (*moves away from door just as the pairs run into the room*)

WILLIAM. (*as soon as both couples are in room*) *Freeze!* (*they continue running*) *This is William Weldon speaking! Everyone freeze!* (*they continue running*)

NATALIE. (*looks at gun, then points it at ceiling and fires*) *Freeze, dirtballs!* (*EVERYONE freezes, including WILLIAM*) I always wanted to say that.

SHEILA. (*looks ceilingward*) Is there anybody *living* up there?

KRIS. Not any more!

WILLIAM. Don't be silly. This is the top floor. Nothing up there but the *roof!*

DAVID. (*panicky*) My *reindeer!*

NATALIE. *"Reindeer?"*

WILLIAM. Natalie, don't be an idiot! Here, give me that thing before you hurt someone. (*takes gun from her*) Now, everyone listen to me! (*picks up sparkly ornament again*) Kris, come over here! (*DAVID crosses to him*) Watch this (*holds ornament in front of DAVID*) and listen only to my voice. When I snap my fingers you are David Tuttle. You love Samantha, your wife. (*Snaps fingers*)

DAVID. (*shakes head then sees SAMANTHA. He rushes to her*) Sam! (*he tries to embrace her*)

KRIS. Wait a minute! What do you think you're doing with my woman? (*he tries to embrace her. SAMANTHA is caught in a tug-of-war. Suddenly DAVID and KRIS toss her to the side and begin wrestling*)

DAVID. She's mine!

KRIS. She's *mine*, I'm David Tuttle!

DAVID. No you're not! *I am!*

WILLIAM. Wait a minute! *Freeze!* (*no response*) I said *stop it!* (*looks at gun in hand. Looks at NATALIE. Shrugs and then fires gun into ceiling*) Freeze, you round pieces of lint! (*DAVID and KRIS stop. NATALIE stares at WILLIAM. He shrugs almost apologetically*)

DAVID. (*looking at ceiling*) I pity anyone on that *roof!*

WILLIAM. David, come here. (*both KRIS and DAVID move to WILLIAM. Then, to DAVID:*) Not you, David. You sit down. (*he sits on sofa. Then, to KRIS*) Now, *you,* David, listen only to my voice. (*Looks around*) And only him! Everyone got that? (*they all nod*) When I snap my fingers you will be Kris Kreigle. And you will be in love with—Sheila! (*snaps fingers*)

KRIS. (*reacts to finger-snap, blinking a bit, then:*) Sheila! I love you!

SHEILA. I know, I know, and I'll write you every day when they send you up the river.

KRIS. What river?

SHEILA. It's an expression. You're going to jail, Kris.

KRIS. Impossible! Nobody would arrest Santa Claus this near to Christmas!

SHEILA. Trust me.

NATALIE. Won't *you* go to jail, too, as an accessory?

DAVID. After all, you're driving the getaway car, aren't you?

SHEILA. No, not *getaway*—*come*-away. Kris always calls when he's at his last job for the night, and then I drive over and say, "Come away, Kris, we'll go home now," and get him into bed with a wet rag on his forehead, and then drop the loot off anonymously at the police station.

SAMANTHA. A fine gun moll *you* are!

SHEILA. If I *was* a gun moll, would I have a regular *day* job?

WILLIAM. Maybe Kris doesn't steal enough to support you?

SHEILA. Of course he does—I just keep returning it.

NATALIE. But *why?* (*when ALL look at her*) I mean— I *know* why—stealing is wrong and crime doesn't pay, but—if he's a burglar, and you're his girl friend ...?

SHEILA. He's *not* a burglar! He really thinks he *is* Santa Claus!

KRIS. *"Thinks?"*

DAVID. Wait a minute, wait a minute! Why would Santa Claus *take* things from people?!

SAMANTHA. Yes, Santa Claus is supposed to *give* gifts, remember?

SHEILA. Ah, but only to *good* little girls and boys! Every time Kris makes a list and checks it twice, everybody on it is *naughty!*

WILLIAM. Fascinating! Absolutely fascinating! I haven't run into a psychosis like this in my entire career! If I could *cure* him, I'd be world-famous!

SHEILA. You're a doctor?

WILLIAM. Better than that: I'm a licensed psychiatrist!

KRIS. I don't want to be treated by a *crazy* doctor!

SAMANTHA. Now-now, nobody said you were crazy.

KRIS. I know that. I mean him.

DAVID. What makes you think *Bill* is crazy?

KRIS. Well, look at the way he *dresses!*

SHEILA. It *is* kinda weird.

NATALIE. (*just noticing*) Bill, why *are* you dressed so weird?

WILLIAM. (*without thinking*) I got dressed in such a hurry ...

SAMANTHA. (*sensing disaster*) Uh, Bill—

DAVID. You know, *I* have clothes that look like that...

KRIS. You're crazy, too?

WILLIAM. (*realizing his peril*) It's *not* what you think, David!

DAVID. I wasn't thinking *anything!*

KRIS. *Told* you he was crazy.

NATALIE. Hold on—*I'm* starting to think something!

SAMANTHA. *No* you're not!

NATALIE. (*as if this were an order, goes blank*) Oh.

WILLIAM. (*hastily, shoving KRIS toward bedroom*) Here, first thing you've got to do is get out of that Santa suit!

KRIS. In front of the ladies?

WILLIAM. No, in the bedroom!

KRIS. But I'm not wearing any underwear!

WILLIAM. There' a blue bathrobe in on the bed.

DAVID. There *is?*

SAMANTHA. Bill's just *guessing!*

NATALIE. After all, David, you have one just *like* that! You were wearing it when you and Sam were necking on the *sofa* tonight!

DAVID. We were *what?*

NATALIE. Now, come *on*, David, surely you *remember?*

SAMANTHA. (*desperately*) Whenever he gets romantic, he forgets things!

DAVID. I do not!

SHEILA. How do you *know?*

(*DAVID goes blank.*)

KRIS. She's got you *there!*

NATALIE. Now, just a minute—if that wasn't *David* necking with Sam, then who—?

SAMANTHA. Of *course* it was David!

DAVID. But I only just *got* here!

WILLIAM. (*trying to get off the topic*) Kris, get into that bedroom and undress!

KRIS. (*heading into bedroom*) I thought you were only going to examine my *head?!*

DAVID. Bill, *can't* you conduct your business in your *own* bedroom?

NATALIE. (*starts for hall door*) Maybe never *again* ... if *his robe* isn't in *our* closet!

WILLIAM. Darling, wait, I can explain!

SHEILA. Explain *what?*

KRIS. (*off, in bedroom*) I can't find the light switch!

WILLIAM. (*by reflex*) It's on the wall to your right! (*realizes, says frantically to NATALIE:*) I *suppose!*

DAVID. Sam, what goes *on* here when I'm working late at the office?

SAMANTHA. (*furiously*) Don't you mean when you're *not* working late at the office?

DAVID. (*caught*) What are you talking about?

SAMANTHA. As if you didn't know! I *phoned* the office tonight!

DAVID. (*bravado*) Checking *up* on me?!

SAMANTHA. I was not!

DAVID. Then why did you phone?

SAMANTHA. (*at lung-top:*) To *apologize* for ever *distrusting* you!

DAVID. (*weakly*) Oh. Good reason.

NATALIE. Sam, there's a perfectly good reason David wasn't there!

WILLIAM. You *knew* he wasn't there?!

NATALIE. Oops!

SHEILA. (*uncertainly*) Are *you* people sure you can straighten *Kris* out?

DAVID. Actually, there's a *reason* I wasn't at the office, Sam.

SAMANTHA. *What* reason?

DAVID. (*opens his mouth, hesitates, then says*) I can't tell you.

NATALIE. David, you've *got* to tell her!

WILLIAM. Natalie—*you* know where he was?

NATALIE. (*opens her mouth, hesitates, then says:*) I can't tell you.

SAMANTHA. Natalie, I thought you were my best friend!

NATALIE. I was! (*then, quickly:*) I mean, I *am!*

WILLIAM. Then what are you and David *keeping* from us?!

DAVID. (*defensively*) What are you and *Sam* keeping from *us?*

WILLIAM. (*opens mouth, hesitates, then says:*) I can't tell you!

SAMANTHA. But we're *not* having an *affair!*

DAVID. Who said you *were?*

SAMANTHA. (*slumps*) *Somebody* would sooner or later!

SHEILA. Maybe I'd better take Kris to a *different* psychiatrist!

SAMANTHA. But *Bill* is the best you can *get!*

SHEILA. Poor Kris!

(*KNOCK at hall door, simultaneous with:*)

POLICEMAN. (*off*) Open up, this is the police!

ALL. The *police!*

KRIS. (*runs out of bedroom, now in BILL's robe, slippers, etc., heads right for chimney, tries to climb up inside it, on:*) Well, if you'll all excuse me—!

SHEILA. (*grappling with him, pulling him back into room*) Kris, you can't get out *that* way!

KRIS. Why not?

SHEILA. Your reindeer won't recognize you in that bathrobe! (*by the way, KRIS still wears his Santa beard, if nothing else of his original outfit*)

KRIS. They'll surely recognize my voice!

SHEILA. But what if they don't?

POLICEMAN. (*off*) Open this door, in the name of the law!

KRIS. (*starts for chimney again*) Excuse me!

WILLIAM. Kris, you have nothing to fear from the police! You're Santa Claus, remember?

KRIS. The police don't *believe* in Santa Claus!

POLICEMAN. (*off, pounding on door*) Open up, or I'll shoot the lock off!

DAVID. I'd better open up!

NATALIE. But what will you *tell* the policeman?

SAMANTHA. *We* haven't broken any laws, Natalie—*have* we?

POLICEMAN. (*off*) I'm going to count to three! One ... two ... !

DAVID. I'm *coming*, I'm *coming*!

SHEILA. You won't turn Kris *in*, will you?

WILLIAM. He's perfectly *safe* not wearing his *Santa* suit!

SAMANTHA. If the policeman doesn't ask him his *name!*

POLICEMAN. ...*three!*

DAVID. *Hold* it! (*yanks open door. OFFICER enters, gun in one hand, large gift-wrapped box under his other arm*) Can we help you, Officer?

POLICEMAN. There's been a complaint!

SAMANTHA. Not from *us!*

POLICEMAN. From your neighbors! They heard *shooting* in here!

NATALIE. (*improvising*) You know, so did *we!* Somebody up on the roof was pumping bullets through the ceiling!

WILLIAM. (*jumping on this handy bandwagon*) We're all lucky to be alive.

SAMANTHA. (*catching on, points ceilingward*) Look for yourself!

POLICEMAN. (*looks up*) Those *are* bullet holes! Who's up on that roof?!

KRIS. (*starts ticking names off on his fingers:*) Dasher, Dancer, Prancer—

SHEILA. (*improvising*) It's all right, Grandfather, the little sleigh has gone away now! (*behind KRIS's back, makes forefinger-twirl at temple to clue policeman in*)

KRIS. With no *driver?*

NATALIE. (*desperately*) Now-now, Grandfather, they know the way home.

POLICEMAN. What's going *on* here, anyhow?

KRIS. (*like a person reporting a crime, right to OFFICER*) Someone's been shooting my reindeer in the feet!

POLICEMAN. I thought the shots came from *outside?*

SHEILA. (*desperately*) Well, see, at *that* time, the reindeer were *inside!*

POLICEMAN. Now, just a minute—!

WILLIAM. (*quickly*) Officer, I assure you, it's all right! I'm a licensed psychiatrist, treating this gentleman, so everything's fine, and you can take my word for it!

POLICEMAN. (*looks him up and down; then:*) In *that* outfit?

SHEILA. Say, what's that package, anyhow?

DAVID. (*gloomily*) Probably gift-wrapped handcuffs!

POLICEMAN. No, this was leaning against the door across the hall. Looked expensive, so I thought I'd better take charge of it before somebody swiped it.

SAMANTHA. *(looks at package)* Natalie, have *you* been shopping at Bergdorf-Goodman?!

WILLIAM. Ye gods, I hope *not!*

POLICEMAN. What's this package got to do with *you?*

WILLIAM. *We* live across the hall, officer.

NATALIE. *(reaches)* So if you'll just give me the package—

POLICEMAN. Not till I see some I.D.!

WILLIAM. Don't look at me, these aren't my clothes!

POLICEMAN. Well, that's *one* point in your favor!

DAVID. I resent that!

POLICEMAN. Why?

DAVID. Because they're *my* clothes!

POLICEMAN. Why is your *neighbor* wearing your *clothes?*

DAVID. *(turns to SAMANTHA)* Your turn.

SAMANTHA. Uh. There's a *very* good reason!

NATALIE. *(as if that cleared things up) Now* may I have my package?

POLICEMAN. *(pulling back from her)* Not so fast! I'd better look inside this to make *sure* it belongs to you!

DAVID. *(panic-stricken)* No, *don't!*

SAMANTHA. David, why *shouldn't* he look inside that box?

DAVID. *(Inanely)* Oh—no special reason ...

POLICEMAN. *(has wrapping off, and opens box, now, lifts out gorgeous sable stole)* Wow! This must cost a fortune!

DAVID. *(without thinking)* You're telling me! *(with thinking, to SAMANTHA:)* Otherwise, I'd have no way of knowing!

WILLIAM. *(picks up card which fell from box as fur came out)* Look, it's a card!

NATALIE. (*desperately, suspecting what DAVID's done*) Oh, Bill, you darling! To not only give me a fur stole, but to enclose a *love*-note, too!

WILLIAM. Huh?

POLICEMAN. (*takes card*) Let *me* see that! (*looks at card, read aloud:*) "To the most wonderful woman on the face of the earth with all the love in all my heart!"

SAMANTHA. Oh, Bill, how wonderfully romantic of you!

POLICEMAN. His name is "*Bill?*" Then why is this signed "*David?*"

OTHERS except DAVID. "David?!"

DAVID. (*feebly*) So *many* people at Bergdorf-Goodman can't spell "Bill!"

SAMANTHA. David! You bought a fur stole for Natalie!

DAVID. Only to keep till Christmas.

NATALIE. Indian-giver!

WILLIAM. How *dare* you buy my wife a fur—and then expect to get it *back*, besides!

DAVID. It was to keep for Samantha!

SAMANTHA. Why can't I keep my *own* fur? You think I'm incompetent or something?!

POLICEMAN. If I might interrupt for a moment—

OTHERS. Shut up!

DAVID. Sam, the fur was a *surprise* for you!

SAMANTHA. (*hurt*) It certainly was.

DAVID. I mean, I wanted to watch your *eyes* light up on Christmas morning!

KRIS. Sounds like he planned to plug her into the *tree!*

SHEILA. Well, that'd certainly be a *surprise!*

POLICEMAN. If you people will just calm *down* for a moment—

OTHERS. Shut up!

DAVID. Sam, I bought the fur for *you!*

SAMANTHA. Ha! You can't *afford* sable stoles!

DAVID. I was doing it on *time!*

POLICEMAN. (*suspicious*) *Where* were you doing time?!

KRIS. An obvious criminal type! Do your duty, officer!

SHEILA. Grandfather, will you keep *out* of this?!

WILLIAM. David, how could you *afford* a sable on *your* salary?!

DAVID. I couldn't! That's why I've been holding down *another* job!

SAMANTHA. *What* other job?

DAVID. If you'll just look in that sack—

POLICEMAN. Hold it! Nobody touches anything! *I'll* look in the sack! (*peeks in wrong sack*) *Silverware?*

SAMANTHA. (*looks*) Hey, that's *my* silverware!

DAVID. The *other* sack!

POLICEMAN. (*looks*) Hey, what's this?! (*lifts out Santa suit*) A soggy Santa suit?

SHEILA. How did that get out of the *bedroom?*

KRIS. More important, how'd it get *soggy?*(*confronts DAVID*) If it shrinks, I'm suing you!

DAVID. Damn it, Kris, that's *my* soggy Santa suit!

NATALIE. (*to SAM*) *Now* do you see where he's been every night?

WILLIAM. Hey, how do *you* know where he's been every night?

DAVID. I needed extra *money*, so I thought if I could pull off the *Santa* job—

POLICEMAN. *Aha!* It finally makes sense! (*grabs DAVID's wrist*) You're under arrest!

OTHERS. What for?

POLICEMAN. For being the notorious Santa Claus burglar!

SAMANTHA. Oh, David, why did you do it, why?!

DAVID. I *didn't!*

POLICEMAN. Then what're you doing with a sackful of silverware?!

WILLIAM. Yeah, Dave, how do you explain *that?!*

DAVID. *I* didn't steal it!

NATALIE. How could he? It's *his!*

POLICEMAN. I've *got* it! He was going to sell the stolen silverware to pay for the sable stole!

SAMANTHA. But David, how could we *eat* any more?

SHEILA. In your new sable, he could take you *out* to eat!

DAVID. Damn it, I did not steal *anything!* I am *not* a burglar! I was paying for that sable stole on my Santa Claus salary!

NATALIE. And that's why he wasn't at the *office* nights! Do you *see*, Sam?

KRIS. She's probably his accomplice!

POLICEMAN. *(takes NATALIE's wrist with his free hand)* You have the right to remain silent—

WILLIAM. She's a woman. Fat chance of that.

NATALIE. Bill, *help* me!

WILLIAM. Take your hands off my wife!

SAMANTHA. And off my husband!

POLICEMAN. *(as ALL converge dangerously on him, pulls gun)* Freeze! *(ALL freeze)* Now, calm down while I get some *answers!*

WILLIAM. What good will that do? Questions answered at gunpoint aren't admissible in court.

SHEILA. Maybe he'll put the gun *away* when we get to court.

DAVID. We're not *going* to court! There's been no *crime* committed here tonight!

KRIS. What about shooting my *reindeer?*

POLICEMAN. *Your* reindeer?

SHEILA. Now, now, Grandfather, don't get yourself upset. The nice officer will take care of it.

WILLIAM. (*to SHEILA*) Why don't you take Grandfather into the bedroom? He's had so much excitement, he needs a little rest.

KRIS. But—(*SHEILA puts hand over his mouth and whisks him into bedroom*)

DAVID. (*to NATALIE quietly*) What's that guy doing in *our* bedroom?

SAMANTHA. I don't care *what* he does in our bedroom—as long as *I'm* not in there *with* him!

POLICEMAN. Can anybody explain what the hell's going on here?

NATALIE. Not me.

SAMANTHA. Me neither.

POLICEMAN. (*stares at WILLIAM*) Well?

WILLIAM. I'll do the best I can.

POLICEMAN. Good! Why don't you start by explaining the gun shots and bullet holes.

WILLIAM. Bullet holes—(*thinks; then pleasantly:*) Have you ever wondered what happens to bullets shot into the air? They have got to come to earth somewhere, right? Well, *two* of those bullets that were shot into the air impacted right there in our ceiling! (*points to ceiling*)

POLICEMAN. Then how do you explain the *gunshots* the neighbors heard?

WILLIAM. The sound traveled with the bullets.

POLICEMAN. But they travel at different speeds!

WILLIAM. That's why we heard the *shots*—just as the neighbors did and *then* the bullets impacted.

POLICEMAN. Bullets travel *faster* than sound!

WILLIAM. (*lamely*) My mistake. (*then to others:*) The bullets impacted *first*. Right?

NATALIE. Sure did!

DAVID. Darndest thing!

SAMANTHA. Amazing!

WILLIAM. Officer, I know this all looks a little *strange* ... (*pauses*) Okay, *very* strange. But see, I'm a licensed psychiatrist ...

POLICEMAN. So you told me.

NATALIE. He really *is*. And I'm his wife.

SAMANTHA. And I'm *his* wife. (*indicates DAVID*)

POLICEMAN. Is *he* a licensed psychiatrist too?

SAMANTHA. No!

POLICEMAN. (*to DAVID*) Congratulations!

WILLIAM. Officer, *most* of the confusion here involves my patient, Kris.

POLICEMAN. Grandfather? (*points to bedroom*)

WILLIAM. Right!

POLICEMAN. Whose Grandfather *is* he?

SAMANTHA. (*mysteriously*) *Noooooo*body knooows—!

WILLIAM. I think *I* can explain: It's my misplaced hypnotism!

POLICEMAN. You misplaced your hypnotism? Where?

WILLIAM. (*picks up ornament*) I don't mean *I* misplaced *it*, I mean *it* was accidentally placed on the wrong *subject!* (*dangle-sparkles ornament*) See, I thought Kris was David, and I was trying to get him to give up his burglary—

POLICEMAN. *Aha!* Then David *is* a burglar!

NATALIE. No, Bill only *thought* he was, because he was wearing a Santa suit!

POLICEMAN. (*to DAVID*) If you weren't a burglar, why were you wearing a Santa suit?

DAVID. I wasn't!

POLICEMAN. But *she* said—

SAMANTHA. She meant *Kris* was wearing a Santa suit, so naturally Bill thought he was *David!*

POLICEMAN. But why would he think that if David *isn't* a burglar?

WILLIAM. Because *I* thought David *was!*

NATALIE. *Now* do you see?

POLICEMAN. Not—even—*slightly!* Let's start at the beginning: Tell me *exactly* what you did ...

WILLIAM. (*dangles ornament before POLICEMAN's face*) Do you see this ornament, officer?

POLICEMAN. Very pretty. What about it?

WILLIAM. Well, when I confronted Kris in the Santa suit, erroneously thinking he was David in his burgling outfit, I said, "Watch this, and listen only to my voice! When I snap my fingers, you are David Tuttle! You are madly in love with Samantha, your wife!" Do you understand?

POLICEMAN. (*in trance-like voice*) I un-der-stand ...

DAVID. Oh, hell, Bill now you've put the *policeman* under!

NATALIE. Wait, it's perfectly okay unless he snaps his fingers!

WILLIAM. But I can't just *leave* him like this!

SAMANTHA. (*shrugs*) Why *not?* It solves all our *problems!*

(*SHEILA and KRIS—he no longer wearing beard—re-enter from bedroom at this point*)

SHEILA. What's going on? Why does that cop look so glassy-eyed?

DAVID. Bill accidentally hypnotized him.

KRIS. (*elated*) Then he can't *arrest* me! Yippee! (*does happy fandango-step, and of course at proper moment does overhead finger-snaps, and:*)

POLICEMAN. *(Breaks from trance, grabs SAMANTHA in his arms) I LOVE YOU! (SAMANTHA screams)*
OTHERS. Oh, noooo!

CURTAIN

End of Act II

ACT III

SCENE: *The same. About an hour later. KRIS is again wearing his Santa suit, but beard is simply tucked into his belt; BILL is once more in his robe, slippers, etc., presumably having returned DAVID's mismatched clothing to the bedroom closet; POLICEMAN sits on floor like rag doll [legs splayed out before him, arms limp with hands loosely on floor between legs, head lolling to one side, eyes glassy, dopey smile on face] at foot of Christmas tree; sacks are gone; SAMANTHA is not onstage; BILL is seated center of sofa, flanked by SHEILA and NATALIE, while DAVID sits on one sofa-arm and KRIS on the other; all five have drinks in hand, and will sip at them now-and-again during dialogue, looking semi-relaxed but intensely thoughtful.*

SHEILA. How long will he *stay* in that trance, Bill?

WILLIAM. Till somebody snaps their fingers.

NATALIE. (*to KRIS*) So, easy on the frenzied footwork, fella.

KRIS. Gotcha.

DAVID. But we can't just *leave* him sitting there!

NATALIE. It's as good a plan as *any* ...

SHEILA. Maybe if you draped him with an afghan ...

WILLIAM. Look, putting him under hypnosis again was just a *temporary* expedient, till we can figure out our next move!

KRIS. I suggest a move to another town.

DAVID. Easy for *you* to say! You don't have a job, a bank account, car payments—

SHEILA. *I* do. If *I'm* willing to move to another town, why aren't *you?!*

NATALIE. David's not a fugitive from justice.

KRIS. He *will* be when that cop snaps out of it.

(SAMANTHA enters from the kitchen, carrying drink; she still wears red pajamas and that Santa cap, but now also wears sable stole, which she caresses lovingly with free hand)

SAMANTHA. Anybody *else* want a refill?

NATALIE. *(motions with drink)* I can hardly concentrate on *this* one!

WILLIAM. Come on, people, *think!* What the hell are we going to do with this *policeman?*

SAMANTHA. Maybe if we explained to him, real nice—

DAVID. We *tried* that, and matters only got *worse!*

KRIS. How about if Bill hypnotizes him to *forget* everything that happened here tonight?

SHEILA. Hey, *that's* not a bad idea!

DAVID. How about it, Bill?

NATALIE. *Could* you?

WILLIAM. Impossible! Even the *strongest* trance wears off naturally after a time—usually overnight!

DAVID. Then maybe we'd *better* start packing!

SAMANTHA. Aw, David, I just finished putting the silverware *back!*

SHEILA. It's very nice of you not to press charges about that.

KRIS. But what if Bill *can't* cure me of burgling places?

SAMANTHA. We *still* can't press charges without untrancing that *cop*—and that's the *last* thing we want to happen!

NATALIE. Look—*maybe* we could—even if the trance *won't* last forever—*maybe* we could arrange it so that cop snaps out of it someplace *else!* I mean, he doesn't *have* to be *here!*

DAVID. What good would *that* do? He can surely find his way *back* here!

SAMANTHA. With a SWAT team!

WILLIAM. I'm *thinking*, I'm *thinking!*

KRIS. Wait, let's be logical. If the cop wakes up, we've had it—

SHEILA. Because he'll put us all under arrest—

NATALIE. For trifling with a police officer in the course of his duty—

DAVID. Aiding and abetting a known burglar—

SAMANTHA. Lying about those gunshots—

WILLIAM. Conspiring to incapacitate an armed lawman—

KRIS. Endangering helpless reindeer—

OTHERS. Oh, cut that out!

DAVID. Well, so much for the *logical* approach! What's left?

SAMANTHA. The *illogical* approach?

NATALIE. You think we should come up with a *stupid* plan?!

SHEILA. A stupid plan is better than no plan at all!

KRIS. Bill, you're a psychiatrist—what *would* be a stupid plan?

WILLIAM. The *best* one so far is Natalie's—have the cop snap out of it someplace *else!*

NATALIE. Thank you, darling!

DAVID. But *where* else?

SAMANTHA. Yeah, *where* could he snap out of his trance so he'd no longer be a *menace* to us?

KRIS. (*snaps fingers as idea hits him; POLICEMAN awakens, but OTHERS don't notice*) The *lion's* cage at the *zoo!*

SHEILA. But the poor man might be *devoured!*

KRIS. Yeah, but they couldn't blame *us* for that!

WILLIAM. No. I draw the line at murdering policemen.

SAMANTHA. But it's only *one* policeman. And maybe he *wouldn't* be devoured, even!

DAVID. We could leave him his *gun*—that way, he'd have a fighting chance, at least ...

(*On "gun" word, POLICEMAN reacts, looks— and sure enough, it's back in his holster; carefully, so as not to be noticed, he starts to reach for it, and:*)

SAMANTHA. Wait! (*snaps fingers as she shouts, and POLICEMAN becomes "rag doll" again*) It doesn't *have* to be something *lethal*, like the *lion's cage!* We could put him on a one-way flight to South Africa, or—

WILLIAM. Be careful what you say, Sam! In his present trance-state, he's very suggestible!

KRIS. You mean he might do what we say, without our even knowing it?

WILLIAM. That's the way hypnotism *works:* You get a person looking at something bright and shiny, with fully focused attention, and pretty soon, whatever they're told to do, they *do!*

SHEILA. You've just described a *television* commercial!

WILLIAM. Why do you think they're so *successful?!*

NATALIE. Good grief, do those TV ad-men *know* that?

WILLIAM. Fortunately not. Otherwise, the messages by political candidates would say, "You *will* vote for Dukakis!"* And everybody *would!*

DAVID. Bill, that's positively terrifying!

SAMANTHA. Let's hope those ad men never find *out* about it!

NATALIE. Say, Sam, wouldn't you like to sit *down?*

SAMANTHA. I don't want to mat the fur. (*happily caresses sable*) Besides, I'm waiting for the dryer to buzz.

DAVID. I sure hope my Santa suit doesn't *shrink!*

KRIS. You can always sell it to an elf.

NATALIE. (*to KRIS, fascinated*) You find life's problems very *simple,* don't you!

SHEILA. Of course he does. He doesn't have to do anything but get *into* trouble! Getting him *out* of it is *my* job!

WILLIAM. Let's concentrate on our *combined* troubles, shall we? We have us a comatose *policeman* on our hands—we certainly can't *kill* him, and we *dare* not wake him *up,* but we can't just leave him under the Christmas tree *indefinitely!*

KRIS. How about we lock him in a closet, slip food under the door, let him out for exercise on national holidays—

NATALIE. That'd never work. Food wouldn't *fit* under a closet door.

KRIS. What about *pizza* ... or *tortillas?*

SHEILA. He might not *like* spicy food.

DAVID. Okay then: We give him a hypnotic suggestion to go to the police commissioner's house and make a pass at his wife! He gets caught, fired from the force, and we're home free!

---

*Note: At premiere, William named a local politician and got a huge laugh; feel free to do likewise.

WILLIAM. The police commissioner's a bachelor.

SHEILA. So how about we hypnotize the police commissioner to fall in love and get married, and as soon as he does, we have the policeman follow him on his honeymoon, and—

KRIS. If it's not a whirlwind courtship, the policeman could die of old age!

WILLIAM. And how could I get *in* to hypnotize the police commissioner in the *first* place?!

NATALIE. The *mayor* has a wife! Why don't we send the policeman over *there*, and—

DAVID. He wouldn't make a pass at *her*. Have you ever *seen* her?!

SAMANTHA. Okay, so why don't we go back to *my* plan, and put him on a plane to South Africa?

WILLIAM. I must admit, it's the best plan so far.

NATALIE. A *boat* to South Africa would be better.

KRIS. A *slow* boat.

SHEILA. A slow *leaky* boat.

DAVID. (*snaps fingers*) *Wait!* (*POLICEMAN un-ragdolls, slowly starts to reach for gun again*) Not South Africa! ... *Russia!*

NATALIE. With a *bomb* in his suitcase!

SAMANTHA. And a map of the *Kremlin* in his pocket!

SHEILA. And a list of the names of all the *politburo* members!

KRIS. His future wouldn't be worth *that!* (*snaps fingers on final word; POLICEMAN ragdolls again*)

WILLIAM. But where do we get the *bomb?*

NATALIE. We could rent a video of *Heaven's Gate!*

SAMANTHA. Or *Ishtar!*

WILLIAM. Be serious, will you? We have a real problem here!

DAVID. Besides, by the time we got the tape, the cop would have come to, arrested us, sent us up the river, and we'd already be eligible for parole.

WILLIAM. You're a *big* help!

SHEILA. (*snaps fingers on:*) I've got it! (*POLICEMAN un-ragdolls, reaches for gun*) You can hypnotize him to *forget* what's happened here tonight!

KRIS. Why didn't *I* (*snaps fingers on pronoun; POLICEMAN ragdolls again*) think of that! It's so simple an *idiot* could have thought of it!

NATALIE. So why *didn't* you?

KRIS. Now, listen—

SHEILA. Calm down, Kris. After all, you *are* an idiot.

KRIS. Oh, yeah, I forgot.

DAVID. So come on, Bill, start the hypnosis!

WILLIAM. *All* of you calm down! Haven't you been paying attention? All post-hypnotic suggestions are *temporary! Sure* I can make him forget ... *today*. But, by tomorrow morning he'll *forget* what he forgot, and we're right back in the soup!

NATALIE. So what's Plan *B?*

WILLIAM. I don't *have* one!

SHEILA. So we may as well go with Plan *A*, right?

SAMANTHA. We couldn't be any *worse* off.

WILLIAM. Oh ... all right! But I'm just saving us temporarily, I warn you! David, Kris, bring the guy over here. (*KRIS and DAVID obligingly pick up POLICEMAN and tote him to center of sofa, where they plop him down, while WOMEN move up in back of sofa to observe matters*) There, that's good enough. Now stand back—and if you don't mind, *please* try to avoid being hypnotized *yourselves!*

DAVID. How do we do *that?*

WILLIAM. Put your hands over your ears, and do *not* look directly at the twinkling *ornament!* Everybody *got* that?

OTHERS. (*have covered ears, so do not hear him, and speak in unison:*) *WHAT?*

WILLIAM. Never mind, never mind, it's just fine, keep covered.

OTHERS. (*simultaneously uncovering*) *WHAT?*

WILLIAM. I said, *cover your ears!*

OTHERS. Oh! (*re-cover ears*)

WILLIAM. (*muttering*) Bunch of idiots—! (*then he holds up ornament before POLICEMAN's face, and:*) Officer, I want you to listen to my voice. Listen carefully to what I am going to tell you. You will follow these directions completely. When you awake you will not remember what has happened in this apartment.

POLICEMAN. (*"Zombie"-type voice.*) I will not remember what has happened in this apartment.

WILLIAM. You will not remember being hypnotized.

POLICEMAN. I will not remember being hypnotized.

WILLIAM. Have you got all that?

POLICEMAN. Have I got all that?

WILLIAM. No-no, I want you to answer me!

POLICEMAN. You want me to *answer* you!

WILLIAM. (*slumps wearily*) This isn't working well at all. (*OTHERS sense his mood of dejection, and uncover ears, on:*)

POLICEMAN. This isn't working out well at all.

SHEILA. *What* isn't?

NATALIE. He's *under*, isn't he?

WILLIAM. For the time being, yes.

SAMANTHA. Then, why isn't this working?

WILLIAM. He keeps *repeating* anything I say to him, even when I don't *want* him to!

SAMANTHA. Why not *tell* him to stop repeating you?

WILLIAM. Never *thought* of that! Worth a try. Officer, you will *stop* repeating everything I tell you!

POLICEMAN. I will *stop* repeating everything you tell me.

WILLIAM. (*to OTHERS, a growl of rage:*) He's doing it *again!*

POLICEMAN. I'm doing it *again!*

NATALIE. Here, now, Bill, let *me* have a try!

WILLIAM. How *can* you? He only hears the sound of *my* voice!

NATALIE. Well, tell him to only hear the sound of *mine!*

SHEILA. *That* sounds logical.

KRIS. (*nods*) Makes sense to *me!*

DAVID. It *must* be okay if even *Kris* gets it!

KRIS. What do you mean *"even"* Kris?!

SAMANTHA. Hush-hush, *all* of you, or we'll *never* get this done with!

WILLIAM. Right! Very well, now—here goes: Officer, from now on, you will hear only the sound of *Natalie's* voice!

POLICEMAN. Which one is Natalie?

WILLIAM. (*points*) *She* is.

DAVID. He can't *hear* you, Bill.

SHEILA. *If* you've done it right.

KRIS. But how can we find *out?*

SAMANTHA. (*shrugs*) Have *Natalie* speak to him!

WILLIAM. Of course! Natalie—?

NATALIE. Officer—can you hear me?

POLICEMAN. Are you Natalie?

NATALIE. Yes, I am.

POLICEMAN. Then I can hear you.

SHEILA. Perfect! Now tell him to *forget* everything, Natalie!

NATALIE. I want you to forget *everything!*

POLICEMAN. All right.

WILLIAM. This is too easy. Test him. Make *sure* he's forgotten everything.

NATALIE. Okay ... Who *are* you?

POLICEMAN. Strange ... I have no idea who I am ... or *where* I am.

SHEILA. It worked!

POLICEMAN. Do *you* know who I am?

DAVID. Is he asking *me*?

WILLIAM. Can't be. He can't *hear* you, only Natalie.

NATALIE. Then let *me* answer: No. We've never met you before.

POLICEMAN. Then what am I doing here? Why am I in this uniform? Am I a cop?

NATALIE. (*panicky*) *No!*

POLICEMAN. Then what am I doing in this uniform?

WILLIAM. Be careful how you answer him!

DAVID. Say this is a masquerade!

SAMANTHA. No, he'll wonder why the *rest* of us aren't in costume!

SHEILA. But we've *got* to explain that uniform *somehow!*

KRIS. Tell him he's the *milkman!*

SHEILA. A milkman with a badge and a gun?!

KRIS. Protection against *milk*-thieves!

WILLIAM. This is *stupid!*

NATALIE. Wait a minute, *I've* got it! ... You are "Pete the Partyin' Policeman"—it's only a costume you're wearing—you came here to—to—(*inspired*)—deliver a strip-a-gram!

KRIS. I don't think Rudolph would approve!

SAMANTHA. What's wrong? Is old "Red-Nose" a blue nose?

POLICEMAN. Where's the *music?*

NATALIE. There *is* music! Listen! Listen hard...!

POLICEMAN. (*cocks his head, and then he—and we [via your sound technician]—hear strains of JAZZY MUSIC, softly at first, then loudening bit by bit, during:*) Ah! Yes! *Now* I hear it! (*starts to dance, slowly at first, then more wildly as MUSIC-VOLUME increases*) How am I doing?

NATALIE. Beautifully!

WILLIAM. Natalie, have you lost your *mind?!*

SAMANTHA. Don't bother her, she's on a roll!

SHEILA. But he's just *dancing*—why isn't he *stripping?*

KRIS. Sheila, what's come *over* you?!

DAVID. Don't answer that—there may be *children* eavesdropping!

WILLIAM. Ladies, control yourselves! Let's not get ourselves into *deeper* trouble!

NATALIE. Bill, we're just trying to have a little fun. (*to SAMANTHA*) Have *you* ever seen a male stripper before?

SAMANTHA. No ... but I've always sorted of *wanted* to—!

DAVID. *Sam!* What are you saying?!

KRIS. Seems clear enough to *me!*

SAMANTHA. Go, boy, go!

SHEILA. He can't hear you!

NATALIE. Oh *I* can fix *that* ... from now on, you hear only the *women's* voices!

WILLIAM. Have you ladies gone bananas?!

SAMANTHA. Get that shirt off!

DAVID. (*as dancing POLICEMAN obliges*) Sam, this is a side of you I've never *seen* before!

NATALIE. (*re POLICEMAN*) And a side of *him* that *we've* never seen before!

WILLIAM. Natalie, this has gone far enough!

SHEILA. It has not—he's still got his *pants* on!

POLICEMAN. (*still dancing*) Sorry! (*starts removing pants, revealing un-police-like shorts [perhaps his drawers have large red hearts, or drawing of Donald Duck; whatever]*) Is that better?

SAMANTHA. Better all the time!

DAVID. *Stop* this! Sam, this is neither the time nor the place for—

SAMANTHA. (*logically*) Do *you* want to explain the uniform to him?

DAVID. Uh—well—if you put it *that* way ...

POLICEMAN. (*now dancing about in his undershorts*) Why am I taking my clothes off?

NATALIE. Because you're delivering a strip-a-gram!

POLICEMAN. I mean, what's the *occasion?*

SHEILA. A *birthday* party!

POLICEMAN. *Whose* birthday?

SAMANTHA. Bill's!

WILLIAM. Hey, now, *wait* a minute—! (*but now POLICEMAN is dancily "vamping" WILLIAM 'round and 'round him, trailing his fingers alongside his face as he circles him, etc.*) Natalie, this is *not funny!*

NATALIE. (*NATALIE and SAMANTHA and SHEILA howling with amusement*) That's what *you* think!

KRIS. It's too bad we haven't got a *video* camera!

DAVID. You're *enjoying* this?!

KRIS. No, I mean, if we got the cop in his underwear on *tape*, we could *blackmail* him into not arresting us!

WILLIAM. Hey! That's *it!* We're home free!

DAVID. We don't *have* a video-camera!

WILLIAM. We don't *need* one!

OTHERS except POLICEMAN. *Whaaat—?!*

WILLIAM. Natalie, *stop* him! I can't *think* while he's coming *on* to me—!

NATALIE. Oh ... (*glumly*) All*ll* right—*Freeze*, buddy! (*POLICEMAN stops dance, and MUSIC stops immediately*) So what' s your plan?

WILLIAM. Gather 'round me, everybody!

NATALIE. You've thought of a plan? (*SHE and OTHERS gather eagerly around WILLIAM, POLICEMAN just stands wherever he was when stopped*)

WILLIAM. (*proudly*) A *foolproof* plan! That cop will never bother any of us again!

KRIS. (*gleefully*) You *are* gonna bump him off?

WILLIAM. Of course not!

KRIS. Aw, shucks.

SHEILA. Kris, darling, if you'd shut *up* we could *hear* Bill's plan!

SAMANTHA. But what *possible* plan? You said posthypnotic suggestions don't *last!*

DAVID. Yeah, he'll remember *everything* by tomorrow morning!

WILLIAM. Yes, but what if there's nothing *to* remember?!

NATALIE. Huh? I don't *get* it?!

WILLIAM. He can't remember something that never actually *happened*, can he?

DAVID. I—I guess not—but—

SAMANTHA. —So many things *did* happen, Bill ...

WILLIAM. Look, will you *listen* to my plan or *won't* you?!

KRIS. Do we have a choice?

WILLIAM. *No!*

SHEILA. So okay, what's your plan?

WILLIAM. First of all—Natalie, will you *please* give the mind-control power back to *me?*

NATALIE. But we were having such *fun* ...!

WILLIAM. Listen, we've been making so much noise the neighbors may call *another* cop, and *then* what'll we do?!

SAMANTHA. He's right, Nat.

NATALIE. Oh ... Okay. (*To POLICEMAN*) From now on, you will hear only the sound of *Bill's* voice, Officer, understand?

POLICEMAN. I understand.

NATALIE. (*to WILLIAM*) He's all yours.

WILLIAM. Good! Officer—you will hear *nothing* that I say to these *other* people, get me?

POLICEMAN. Gotcha.

WILLIAM. Okay, gang, here's the plan: David, do you have any spackle?

KRIS. It doesn't work as well as cement.

SHEILA. We are *not* dropping the cop into the *river!* (*to WILLIAM, less certainly:*) Are we?

NATALIE. We'll never get *anywhere* the way *Kris* keeps interrupting!

WILLIAM. I've taken *that* into consideration, too! Now, David—?

DAVID. Yes, there's a box of spackle under the kitchen sink.

WILLIAM. Good. Get it out, mix up a small batch, and you and Sam get the step stool and start filling in those *bullet*-holes up there!

SAMANTHA. Right! (*SHE and DAVID exit to kitchen*)

WILLIAM. Now, Natalie, do you have a dancing-gown that'll fit Sheila?

NATALIE. A *dancing-gown?*

WILLIAM. Do you or don't you?

NATALIE. Why—yes, I have. Why?

WILLIAM. Take her across to our place and get her into it.

SHEILA. But *why* do you want her to take me and—?

WILLIAM. *Move!*

NATALIE. Yessir, right away, on the double! (*salutes, and SHE and SHEILA exit to hall*)

KRIS. And what do you want *me* to do?

WILLIAM. (*places hand firmly upon his shoulder*) You are coming with *me* into the *bedroom!*

KRIS. (*as WILLIAM guides him toward door*) What about the cop?

WILLIAM. He'll keep!

KRIS. But—Bill—what are you going to do? I don't like that look in your eyes ...

WILLIAM. I am going to erase that Santa-Claus-burglar obsession from your mind *forever!*

KRIS. But you said hypnosis doesn't *last!*

WILLIAM. I was talking about a *normal* person's mind! Remember—*you* are an *idiot!*

KRIS. (*with big beatific smile*) Lucky me! (*Then, just before entering bedroom, stops and turns to BILL, for:*) But—if you alter my Santa-Claus-personality—

WILLIAM. Yes ...?

KRIS. (*very bewildered*) Where will I *go?* What will I *do?*

WILLIAM. (*a la Rhett Butler:*) Frankly, my dear, I don't *give* a damn! (*shoves KRIS ahead of him into bedroom, shuts door after them*)

DAVID. (*entering with step stool from kitchen*) Hurry up with that spackle! It's spooky being alone here with the Living Statue! (*will set stool up beneath "bullet holes" and get onto it, balancing carefully*) I wish I knew what good plugging those *holes* is going to do!

SAMANTHA. (*entering with very small bowl of spackle and putty knife*) I'm sure he had a good *reason*, David. Be careful—I don't want you to fall!

DAVID. (*taking bowl and knife from her*) That makes two of us! (*will start to plug "holes" [i.e.: make "spackling-motions" toward wherever ceiling in normal room would be]*)

SAMANTHA. I wonder where everybody *else* has got to?

WILLIAM. (*leans head out of bedroom*) Sam! Get seven drinking-glasses and put ice in them!

SAMANTHA. This is no time to *party*, Bill!

DAVID. He didn't say *liquor*, he said *ice!*

SAMANTHA. Oh—all right! (*exits to kitchen*)

DAVID. (*spackling away*) Bill, I wish you'd let us *in* on your plan!

WILLIAM. No time now, I'm busy with Kris's mind!

DAVID. *That* shouldn't keep you very long!

WILLIAM. Ho-ho, very funny! (*re-exits to bedroom, shuts door again*)

DAVID. Say, this stuff covers the bullet holes just fine!

SAMANTHA. (*off*) That's nice to know if we ever get into the *saloon*-repair business.

WILLIAM. (*leans out bedroom door*) On second thought, put *liquor* in those glasses!

SAMANTHA. (*off*) Bill, this is getting expensive.

WILLIAM. Not as expensive as hiring a defense attorney!

SAMANTHA. (*off*) You've made your point.

WILLIAM. Good! (*Re-exits to bedroom, shuts door*)

NATALIE. (*enters from hall*) Well, here's the dancing-girl!

SHEILA. (*enters in a rather flamboyant dance costume—frills, spangles, etc.*) Ta-daaa!

DAVID. Just where *do* you go dancing, Natalie—Radio City Music Hall?

NATALIE. I bought it on our vacation in Rio. It looked *normal* down *there!*

SHEILA. Where's Kris?

SAMANTHA. (*entering with tray of seven drinks*) Getting exorcised in the bedroom.

NATALIE. What're the *drinks* for?

SHEILA. Yeah, it's a bit premature to *celebrate!*

DAVID. (*finished, coming down from step stool*) Not to mention Bill included a drink for that *cop*, besides.

SAMANTHA. What's the *cop* going to celebrate?

DAVID. (*taking bowl, knife and step stool out to kitchen*) I don't want to *think* about it.

NATALIE. Are we allowed to *drink* those drinks?

SAMANTHA. That's not the *worst* suggestion of the evening! (*sets down tray, and WOMEN each pick up a glass*) But maybe we should *ask* Bill about it, first ...?

SHEILA. There's a time for asking, and a time for drinking!

NATALIE. Right on! (*SHE and SHEILA drain about half their drinks, in unison*)

SAMANTHA. Oh, well, there's more where *this* came from! (*drains half her own drink, during:*)

DAVID. (*re-entering from kitchen*) Not *much* more! Did you have to use the *good* scotch?!

NATALIE. You mean you don't *want* yours?

DAVID. (*picking up glass*) Try and stop me! (*drains half his drink as WILLIAM enters*)

WILLIAM. I made a mistake! We only need *six* drinks!

DAVID. Then I'll get rid of *this* one! (*finishes drink, heads for kitchen*)

SHEILA. So the cop *doesn't* get a drink?

WILLIAM. Of *course* he does! *Kris* doesn't.

NATALIE. Where *is* Kris, anyhow?

WILLIAM. In a deep trance. If I did it right, when he comes out of it, he'll never be Santa Claus again!

SHEILA. I wish you'd waited till *after* Christmas! He was very generous.

WILLIAM. Wouldn't you rather have him a *normal* man?

SAMANTHA. You man "stingy?"

DAVID. (*returning from kitchen minus glass, and taking a fresh drink from tray*) Sam, be fair! *I'm* a normal man, and that sable stole cost an arm and a leg!

NATALIE. It *is* lovely, Samantha.

SAMANTHA. Yeah, but somehow, I thought I'd wear it for a more festive occasion than helping to spackle a ceiling!

WILLIAM. Never mind about that now! Let's get my *plan* into action!

SHEILA. Fine by me. What *is* your plan?

WILLIAM. (*beckons group into huddle*) Come here, everyone, and I'll *tell* you! (*lowers voice, but talks to football-huddled co-conspirators; we cannot hear his words, but during his spiel, the following four interjections are made, with short spiel-bits in-between:*)

NATALIE. Why, Bill, that's positively *brilliant!*

SHEILA. But will it *work?*

DAVID. Seems pretty logical to *me!*

SAMANTHA. I'm not sure I *understand* the plan ...?!

WILLIAM. (*Breaks from spieling, and GROUP un-huddles a bit, on:*) It's *got* to work! Remember, it's what *didn't* happen to that cop that he'll never be able to *recall*, don't you see?

NATALIE. Well, I'm game if you are.

WILLIAM. Does everybody know what they're supposed to do and say?

SAMANTHA. I *think* so ...

SHEILA. But shouldn't we have some *music?* (*starts moving toward POLICEMAN*)

WILLIAM. The music supposedly has *just ended* when I snap him out of his freeze.

SHEILA. (*right in front of POLICEMAN now*) Fair enough. Let's get started.

WILLIAM. Okay! (*To POLICEMAN*) Officer, do you see that girl in front of you?

POLICEMAN. I see the girl.

WILLIAM. Take her into your arms. (*POLICEMAN does so*) Now bend her way backwards.

NATALIE. Not *too* far, the seams will split!

SAMANTHA. Don't *confuse* the man!

DAVID. She can't; he only hears *Bill's* voice. (*POLICEMAN bends SHEILA backward*)

WILLIAM. Okay, everybody—this is *it!* You all know your parts?

OTHERS except POLICEMAN. Right!

WILLIAM. Then here goes nothing! (*braces himself, then snaps fingers. POLICEMAN comes to, reacts to SHEILA with astonishment, then double-reacts as OTHERS start lusty applause.*)

NATALIE. That was wonderful!

SAMANTHA. So graceful!

DAVID. So macho!

WILLIAM. So professional!

SHEILA. And *super*-romantic! (*kisses still-embracing POLICEMAN on the mouth*)

POLICEMAN. (*breaks away, disengages from her, bewildered*) Hey! What *happened?* What am I *doing!* (*looks down at self in shock*) What am I doing in my *underwear?!*

SHEILA. Giving me tango lessons! You're a marvel!

NATALIE. Can *I* be next?

SHEILA. No way! He's *mine!*

POLICEMAN. (*backing off a step*) The *hell* I am! Where are my pants? Where's my shirt? Where's my *gun?!*

DAVID. Right over there, where you took them off, officer.

SAMANTHA. Where *else* would they be?

POLICEMAN. (*rushes to items, starts putting them on, fast*) I don't know what you people think you're doing, but you're in *big ... trouble!*

WILLIAM. (*innocently*) Trouble? What *for?*

NATALIE. Aren't you going to finish your *drink*, officer?

POLICEMAN. What drink? I never drink on duty!

WILLIAM. (*points to lone drink on tray*) Then what do you call *that?*

SAMANTHA. And since when are you *on duty?*

POLICEMAN. Since I *got* here, to investigate those *shots!*

OTHERS. (*innocently*) What shots?

POLICEMAN. (*points toward ceiling*) The shots that made those *bullet—!* ... Hey, where *are* they?

SHEILA. Where are *what*, darling?

POLICEMAN. The *bullet holes!*... "Darling?!"

OTHERS. *What* bullet holes?

POLICEMAN. (*nearly re-dressed now*) The ones in the *ceiling!* When I came here tonight—

WILLIAM. When you came here, officer, you said it was to investigate some *shots*—

DAVID. —but when we said we didn't *know* anything about any shots—

SAMANTHA. —you decided to join our little *party!*

NATALIE. How many drinks did he *have*, anyhow?

SHEILA. I lost count after the *third* one!

POLICEMAN. I've been *drinking?*

WILLIAM. What's the matter—head kind of fuzzy?

POLICEMAN. It's perfectly *clear*, thank you!

DAVID. So what's your problem?

NATALIE. Oh, by the way, where do you want us to send the *video?*

POLICEMAN. *What* video?

SAMANTHA. Of you teaching Sheila to *tango*, of course!

POLICEMAN. In my *shorts?*

WILLIAM. That part wasn't *our* idea.

SHEILA. You said it was more romantic that way.

DAVID. And was it ever!

POLICEMAN. Now, hold on a minute—!

NATALIE. But where *should* we send it—to your home or to the station house?

POLICEMAN. (*panicked*) *Neither!* My wife would *kill* me?

SHEILA. *Wife?!* You have a *wife?!*

POLICEMAN. Why *shouldn't* I have?

WILLIAM. Because you proposed *marriage* to *Sheila*, that's why!

SAMANTHA. That's the *best* part of the videotape.

POLICEMAN. (*starting to back toward hall door*) You—you have a *videotape* of me—in my *underwear*—proposing *marriage*—and giving *tango* lessons?!

SHEILA. (*weepily, heartbroken*) It was going to be my *engagement* present to you!

POLICEMAN. But I *can't* marry you! I've already *got* a wife!

SHEILA. (*a wail of misery*) Ohhhhh! (*rushes into DAVID's comforting arms*)

NATALIE. You won't get away with this!

WILLIAM. We'll sue you for breach-of-promise!

POLICEMAN. *All* of you?!

DAVID. Why not? We're all *witnesses* to your marriage proposal, Charlie!

POLICEMAN. Who's *Charlie?*

SAMANTHA. You mean you gave us a phony *name*, too?!

POLICEMAN. (*the first ray of hope*) You don't know my *name?*

WILLIAM. We don't *have* to—we can find out from your *badge*-number!

POLICEMAN. Listen, I can't afford a scandal—

NATALIE. Say, what *is* his badge-number?

POLICEMAN. (*hand covering badge immediately*) None of your business!

SHEILA. But——if we don't know his real name or his badge-number—how can we track him down?!

POLICEMAN. (*with giddy laugh of hysterical joy*) You *can't!* (*Gallops out into hall, slamming door behind him, and we hear GALLOPING FOOTFALLS, and his continuous gleeful [almost insane] laughter, both sounds slowly fading away to silence; after a long, tense pause. OTHERS burst into relieved laughter, nearly collapsing with delight; then, after they gain some control of themselves:*)

WILLIAM. *Now* we've *really* got something to celebrate! (*ALL raise glasses*)

DAVID. Here's to no more late nights at the office!

SAMANTHA. And here's to my new sable stole!

NATALIE. And here's to never seeing that *policeman* again!

SHEILA. And here's to Bill, for curing Kris of his *Santa Claus* delusions! (*ALL drink and as they do so, bedroom door opens, and KRIS—in an Easter Bunny suit, carrying a basket full of colored eggs—comes happily hopping out into room, up to hall door, and out into hall and away; OTHERS stare after him for a long moment, then:*)

SHEILA. (*Looks bewildered, then says to SAMANTHA and DAVID:*) You keep an *Easter Bunny* outfit in your bedroom—?!

SAMANTHA/DAVID/NATALIE/WILLIAM. (*pause, unified shrug, then, out front:*) ... Doesn't *everybody?*

CURTAIN

THE END

SET DRESSING

Stockings for the chimney
Couch
Coffee table
Table or desk
Telephone
Small, partially decorated Christmas Tree

PROPS

ACT I:

Boxes of ornaments; Box for Santa suit; 2 Wine glasses; 2
Gift-wrapped boxes; Large plastic bag for Santa suit;
Large plastic bag for silverware; Special hypnotizing
ornament, metallic and multi-faceted

ACT II

2 Guns - one with blanks; Large gift-wrapped box with fur
stole; Card

ACT III

Bowl for spackle; Putty knife; Step-stool; 7 liquor and ice-
filled glasses; tray for glasses; Basket of colored Easter
eggs

"SORRY! WRONG CHIMNEY!"
(alternative stage settings)

[premiere setting]

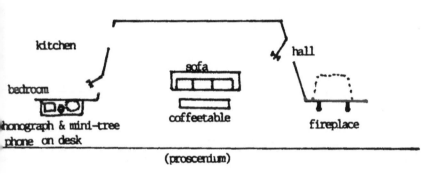

kitchen

hall

sofa

bedroom

phonograph & mini-tree
phone on desk

coffeetable

fireplace

(proscenium)

[ideal setting]

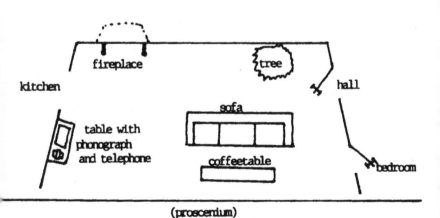

fireplace

tree

kitchen

hall

sofa

table with
phonograph
and telephone

coffeetable

bedroom

(proscenium)